Celebrations

Celebrations

Alan Burns

CALDER

CALDER PUBLICATIONS
an imprint of

ALMA BOOKS LTD
3 Castle Yard
Richmond
Surrey TW10 6TF
United Kingdom
www.calderpublications.com

Celebrations first published in 1967
This edition first published by Calder Publications in 2019

Text © Alan Burns, 1967, 2019

Cover design by Will Dady

Printed in Great Britain by CPI Group (UK) Ltd, Croydon CR0 4YY

ISBN: 978-0-7145-4919-4

Contents

Celebrations

Chapter 1

C ERTAIN ACCIDENTS had culminated in the wash-out of the year. Williams was well equipped in the tone of his impersonal voice; he polished the surface of the desk, nursed his torn arm like a broken engine, prepared for disaster. He was dominated by a mood of simple dread, yet since the machine could be repaired, stored for a year, kept in a shed, his urgency had no meaning. The breakup of his team of men worried him too; he was a gambler waiting for something to snap, for success or failure – it was a matter of routine. A diffident, unimaginative man, he disliked the phenomenal, moved more delib-erately now, walked down to the factory with his hands behind his back.

"The excess oil disappeared quicker – just over seven hours – fine, fine thank you." The covers were lifted off; Williams stood by the machine, not an ounce of excess flesh on him; the sun gleamed on the heavy oil. He turned the wheel slowly; his temperature and the machine's were taken, his serious brown eyes apart, reading the faintest movement of the quiver-ing needle. The cloud of noise subdued; he had no choice; his two assistants noted the start and finish.

"What do you think of her?" At seven fifteen he disconnected the inlet tubes. After the faulty decision to start the power, the man was a stone lighter. For the third time the hammering had been due to human error. "These machines are all the same. I will build another."

"He was a jaunty man, I remember," they said when he died at sixty-four, his appearance dry and crumbling, his face grey from contusion in the brain.

His buttons still glinted in a neat row, his eyes very blue; there was no point in measuring them; the ruptured middle ear caused tears to run down the cheeks, crystals on wheels. After months of useless work, the most unsuccessful of all time, he lost his nerve. The loss in reputation cost thousands; it was all over. The photographers took pictures – Williams wore one of those shirts made specially for him, the blazer made of blue, his elder son Michael in a suede jacket at his side. Williams described the difficulties, the personal sacrifice, then tendons in his neck; he would end with nothing.

The power was on; Williams turned and grinned. He fixed a baffle plate to prevent buckling; the medallion round his neck swung as he swung the handle; he liked to work in the open air. "Better take a look at that." The opinionated extrovert man had no worry and no doubts – all he said, he was. He averted his eyes from his two sons, who were standing by, fiddling with the wiring inside a home-made slot machine.

Most workers owned motor cars, and at weekends they journeyed to admire the surrounding countryside. Those who stayed behind spent their time playing with the slot machines they had built in their spare time. While they played they had the illusion of travelling abroad – to the tropics and the Arctic, even to Mars. Williams had a sense of humour, and when he saw the men wasting time on these toys he did not register it as a breach of discipline, since it could do no harm for them to play to their hearts' content. As long as they were back by Monday, they were free to travel hundreds of miles – to foreign countries, to the planets. They were not asked where they had been. Such nostalgic links with the exploring tradition were recognized as natural.

Williams took his time. After a last check, the way a mother would look at her child, he walked away, aware not of his technological achievement, but of the need for a show of confidence in his calculations. There was a flaw in the manufacturing process; he thought about it as he walked away – the thought cut him off completely. He went back to test his sons' reactions, to understand their relationship. He decided to complete the job; he needed a new approach; he began to form a series of ideas beyond his control. A plane flew overhead, and plane and man were remote from time and impossible to track.

In the factory forecourt a metal pylon was planted, with a flag at the top. A new piece was added every day, to counteract the feeling that "nothing is reproduced", to help combat nervous strain. Indeed, it became difficult to think of the place without the growing pylon with the flag at the top.

Despite the heat and the cloud cover lowered over, Williams wore his coat. While he strove to create the perfect rhythm of work to be done in any weather, the skilled men considered that their work was produced more by their imagination than by practical effort; if there was any muscular exertion it was not apparent – there was a tendency for sweat to be regarded as an anachronism now; production was becoming no more than a branch of the mathematical sciences. Already the beginnings of unfriendliness appeared everywhere; morale became a substance with a practical use – it was tracked and weighed and reduced to a mark on a graph.

"Do you realize what it means to be involved, responsible for this work?" Williams asked his sons. As far as the elder, Michael, was concerned, it was a bloody place – filthy, something unearthly about it. His brother Phillip crouched over the pinball machine: "I've beaten the record! A hundred and eight!" "Possibly, but what do you think you're doing?" Williams switched off the power; the light was poor and the dim outline of his young son's face winced as Williams held his breath and slammed a steel bar against the glass top of the box. "Will the new prototype be ready on time?" Phillip asked. "It's not my concern – you must see to it," Williams spat the words out. It was more than a matter of time; his was the controlling personality – apart from him there was no point – when he was away the place collapsed. As the bar hit the glass with a crash, Williams muttered, "It's good to see some action." The father smashed up the machine which his sons had taken months to build. "We all had fun with it," Michael said. "There'll be hell to pay from the men." "No doubt, but the thing was a disgrace. It had to be destroyed."

Williams was a man of character. He spun a wheel, then was swallowed up by the machine as he bent over and examined the damage. He stayed there an hour. When he looked up, no one was waiting. He jerked a lever forwards and down. Here the individual could look through his own small window; he could come and go. Williams pondered whether he should show any sign of bitterness; in any event his feelings would count for little. He had worked through the night; the sky was brightening; he seemed to be changing his mind; he went to inspect his son Michael's work. Williams was in the centre of the main assembly room, the size and shape of an aircraft hangar; glass roof let the daylight in; floors connected by metal stairs like fire escapes inside the building; rows of tables beside quiet conveyor belts. One moment Williams was sitting opposite a new machine, then it was a heap of junk. He thought of his sons, Michael and Phillip, and he knew he could work harder than either of them. His responsibilities had held him for twenty-four years – now there was no one waiting.

He took the grey car with the new tyres, drove towards his large green armchair; thinking about the horizon and the glaring parallel along the wall of the eternal, Williams saw the bright circle of the luminous watch made specially for him. On his journey towards the mantelpiece he sang 'Sun and Sky Above'; he reached the arterial road, turned right, towards home, the job complete. He drove down the blue road to the waking town. The factory had once been sited in town, then new buildings had been erected in the fields; now again they were being encroached upon by the expanding town. "That damned man works like a maniac," Michael said in his sleep. The ritual remained unchanged; Williams drove with elation; from the road came the sound, the faint whimper, whistle of poured salt; it will finish.

Williams required total loyalty from his sons. They were his pets – he called them "his animals". They answered to his call with grunts or with effortless gliding, according to his will. He never stopped talking about them. They stayed with him. "This is my family" – puffing his pipe and keeping his secret, a suffocating man who knew where to find oxygen. "Well, what do you think of them?" he stopped in mid-sentence, the linen shirt flapping in the wind.

"A five-pound note to the one who climbs the mast." The two young men raced to the mast, while their father retreated inside the dim green room...

The wind and the sky: these had been the events of the day – there had been no others. When Williams and his wife had arrived in the town, he had not been able to find the street on the map. Ten houses on either side: the houses had three floors, the rooms small. The iron foundry still stood and dominated the street. From the railway the sounds of the trains were part of their dreams. Their neighbours were poor people – five in a room – who watched through windows. Williams at thirty had an ordinary name; tall, with few interests, he worked hard. The mother was a woman who died. They had always lived in even-numbered houses. Michael was a good boy – he enjoyed games, he sang in the choir. Phillip was frailer than his fellows; he swung his arms; the presence of others did not help; smothered, he lacked vitality. Phillip developed a horror of dirt; people noticed it; he felt free when he played in the grave; there were things to see; he feared female magic; photography was Phillip's hobby, and the church; he learnt to dance – a joke he kept to himself. On the right upper arm, five bruises; right buttock raw; true, I beat my son; he broke dishes and stole money. The child under the stairs, his arm up to protect his face; Phillip did not understand the pattern; he kept quiet; he had small feet; his hair was ginger. The house was too small; soft earth outside; the stairs faced the door at right angles to the bedroom – a room above a room; a man of sixty whose eyes were about to fail, who left his room unfurnished...

Williams had started his elder son as a methods engineer. Michael was responsible for the complete free flow along the line; he was father of the product completely. Michael was a man whose eyes missed nothing – nothing which had not already been announced.

Phillip volunteered to work at a great height, in excess of nine thousand feet; attached to his ankle was a meter which gauged his preoccupation with his work; a chronometer recorded the time. During this period, of all the work done in the factory, none was as methodical as his. Then the boy complained that the plastic coat was not thick enough – he felt cold, though his heart thumped with the effort of work. Phillip was removed back to his normal workplace and was seen to benefit from the reassurance of a definite routine. Michael was taken to the centre of the factory and told to avoid exertion. It was noted that between these two extremes a comradeship sprang up – this made for a poor standard of work; the experiment was abandoned.

The main transmission belts and fifty superbly complex machines, if not more, were in Michael's care. At a comparatively low cost he had constructed, to judge by the framework, one of the most hideous gantries in the world. Rust was beginning to erode the base. Michael, who never drank anything, suddenly ordered a beer. His brother brought him a glass of water. The younger brother had always had difficulty in learning obedience. When empty wage packets had been distributed, their contents confiscated by the management, Phillip had been sent to spy on the men's secret meetings in their houses, but had reported back to his father merely: "It needed nerve." Phillip knew he had made another mistake. Michael recognized the strain across the throat, the neck, the face stiff with ugliness, the mouth hidden behind obscure houses. The boy experienced a sharp pain in his eyes when he was sent again with the order written out and the key words underlined. Phillip came back to say he could not find the right room, but his words were cancelled before he had finished speaking when his brother pointed with his foot at the door. In dealing with a younger brother, Michael felt that a hint should be given; a hint was frequently needed.

"This is a significant achievement. I ask for a drink and you bring me nonsense," Michael said, as Phillip arranged the glasses. Michael pointed at his brother, and said loudly: "Now who's that chap? Does he work here?"

The younger brother bent his head. The attitude demanded paralysis, a blow on the back of the neck, but it would have been too costly – the move would have taken up too much time, dislocated work schedules, added unduly to the engineer's excessive responsibilities.

Phillip was trapped by his machine. "You could crush me with a single turn of that wheel," he said to his brother. Then an accident crushed the apathetic boy; he jerked; only the head could move. "What happened?" Blood and the usual gash in the face. "It hurts."

Williams was called; he walked unhurriedly across to his son, busy with his notebook. He leafed through the book, glanced over it and asked Phillip if he would like a game of golf. The boy gave a short laugh, crinkled his eyes with pain. "No, not just now." With his hand Phillip made a gesture to cut his throat: "All I'm fit for." He continued sawing the air with his hand, then his hand slipped to his side. He held a sheaf of papers in a blue folder, which he laid across his face to shield himself from the light Williams played on his eyes with a torch shaped like a pencil. The boy closed his eyes.

Phillip ate and slept clutching a letter from his wife. Although the factory radio broadcast only music, he listened perpetually for news from her. In bed he wore the little conical hat his wife had knitted for him; though it was three years since he had seen her, the network of esoteric memories persisted. He had left her for three months to join a geological expedition and had not returned; every month he applied for his release, and a day later requested that his application be cancelled. Phillip did not take the old letter from its envelope, but spent hours examining the postmark. During a regular monthly period he slept out in the open, and doctors noted that his reactions revealed a clear pattern. He would walk as far as he could in temperatures below zero, then dash back into the warmest part of the factory, trembling. He repeated this game twelve times a year; it became a cliché.

"What are you doing now? Do you want to get me the sack? Would you behave like this at home?" his father asked, pretending to be annoyed; then he moved the folder to one side, and the light darted into the pupil of the left eye. Phillip's expression now showed he was startled; his face twitched; the movement spread to his arms – he jerked the folder out of reach: "Mustn't touch!" Williams played his waiting game while his son held him with his gaze. "Live and let live, Dad. You two go off and play golf or whatever it is."

Except for one or two disconcerting psychiatrists who visited the factory and answered "yes" to every question, no reference was made to the past, and everyone agreed that life was so much more lively now. The new motor cars were seen to be racing about, emphasizing the sterility of the place. Little was said about children: "These matters do come up in discussion, but not often. The men are more spiritual than their fathers ever were."

Then silence – five seconds of it. Williams licked his lips – his tongue slid along the thin dry lips while he watched Phillip fiddle with the buttons of his untidy smelly little jacket. "This is riddle talk; you don't appreciate that I'm merely checking your reflexes – pure routine," Williams said. His eyes probed into the boy.

"You have your trade and I have mine, or so I like to think." He tightened his son's tie, forcing the collar close to the chin. "Must be thorough – can't afford to miss anything, understand?" "This file is full of notes," Phillip said. "If anything happens to me it goes to my wife. I've got witnesses and everything." "Exactly, sir" – from his place at his father's side, Michael bent down to assist his brother hunched in a chair before him – "now, is there anything you need, or would you prefer to be left alone?" Phillip sighed and surrendered, and an hour passed.

Towards March the sun began to shine; those who normally wore coats began to appear without them; there were no other signs of spring to be seen – no birds, no cockroach on the floor. Apart from a couple of mice kept illegally in one of the storage dumps, the men had no pets – neither dogs nor cats. Soon the sun became fainter each day.

Phillip's strained eyes moved slowly and read a word; he looked beyond his brother; the workshop seemed longer than a train – darker, more dramatic. He wanted to dream peacefully for hours, before it became too cold. He tried to speak; his throat caught on a note. The workshop was startled; conversation ceased with a click. From the floor, the menace of a lunatic. Outside, flowers in an oval bed. "There's been a mistake!" From the foot of his machine Phillip looked up at his father. "We pay for a doctor to protect us – why doesn't he come?" "What's wrong now?" Williams asked. The response was a struggle of laughter; Phillip's eyes lowered; the silence held steady. "It's against your interests to make a fuss," Williams said. With a sharp and urgent insult to his father's intelligence, the boy coughed and slid to the floor. He was lifted onto a bench. Williams picked him up and cradled him to his shoulder; the swift professional movement was set and held for the men gathered round. "See that?" one said. "That's enough. There's nothing to see." Michael overheard his father mumble to himself "I said one was enough", and Michael's quick eyes caught the look of help, but he would not chance getting involved by kneeling down and helping to carry Phillip – nor did anyone take the slightest risk of losing a day's pay by being called away altogether.

"It was a hundred to one, sir." The doctor held Phillip's legs to stop him injuring himself. "On the right there is no movement in the lower limb. The leg, or part of it, needs blood. Tomorrow he can have a transfusion; we will have a sample from the wife." The doctor would not use the father's blood without testing it – he could not be sure – he thought the blood groups differed. "We've enough on our plates without taking unnecessary risks." He fiddled with his stethoscope, whistling mournfully, thoughtfully. "Time is short. It would be a pity to waste too much time," Williams said. The doctor said it was a calculated risk – "Something should be done to simplify procedure—" "Save your breath," Williams said. "We'll have plenty of questions now. Don't worry. I'll deal with them."

The doctor was due for his annual holiday; he thought he would profit from the extended leisure – in the daytime anyway. There was a pause; slowly the medical man reckoned on his fingers the vacant days. Like the rest of the factory workers, the doctor contented himself with the usual distractions – good food, nightly movies, the photographs of last summer. Sealed off by routine, two at a time, the men remained at their machines. Family groups, personal messages helped to sustain morale. Their relationships generally were good – more grown-up. None of the men were normally permitted to marry while they worked at the factory, so they thought not of production norms but of fertility figures; they dreamt of the red-haired girl swimming naked in the sea.

In the white room where Phillip was taken – polished and shining, divided into squares – the amputated leg had nothing to hope for. "It is sad; it is the law; it is punishment." The yellow chair with the high back stood as in the family home. The table was built into the wall; the electric door led to the telephone, the plug pulled out. The room was an achievement. Phillip was carried in on a door; the quiet room filled with flowers; he looked triumphant; his legs and hands could not rest – he wanted to touch, to do, everything. Michael returned to the factory cinema, where the latest film was being shown. Alone in the electric room, the boy was teased with needles. The door opened, and the flowers were taken away.

About forty of the skilled workers – those in excellent physical condition – took to sleeping in those parts of the building that were constructed underground. They gave as their reason the need to check that no rats got among the stores.

Phillip developed an obsession with the radio, spending hours at a time hugging it to his body, listening to the everlasting canned music in the hope of hearing his

wife's voice, though he knew that the music was broadcast from a stock of tapes in his father's office and that
the radio was incapable of picking up anything else. The
facts were patiently explained to him, yet he would be
found by the radio each day. Only after some time did
Phillip's understanding return, and he was amused by
his elder brother's description of his behaviour. While
others took to excessive drinking or smoking and barely
noticed the food brought to them, Phillip gradually
became more isolated. He lived for days in the most
savage of all climates: his own imagination. His brother
Michael behaved in a subtle manner; he avoided any
human gathering; he made his journeys alone. At this
stage Phillip appeared so well that the doctors thought
they had found the recipe for rude health; then he began
to speak about the factory in a distant, disconnected
way – that it "had the merit of simple living"; he asked
to be moved to where the surveyors were said to have
discovered rare minerals beneath the ground.

Phillip's mouth slobbered all the time he was feeding it; the thick acute eyes were pale underneath. The
boy continued his bowel movements, and the doctor
said, coming in after a few minutes, after beaming
a bit, "A few glasses of sherry will restore his confidence." Then, "He's going," and called in Phillip's wife
Jacqueline, who roused him and fumbled about at his
side for twenty-four hours. "I'll get it," she said, when
the young head raised and asked for water. So he prepared for the end in pain and isolation – his wife was
brought in as witness to it. Phillip said in a joke that he
wanted her to go first – for someone to go ahead and
prepare the way for him.

Phillip's wife was at his side; she held his arm.
"I forget the time" – her voice as smooth as her face.
"Phillip's shoes are missing; I saw them in his father's
room; they are canvas and very light." Jacqueline stayed
by the bed. For an hour the blue eyes remained as he
had been for days – nil movement, nothing to see;
neither moved – the smile swinging through her lips
became her language. The light was cut from under
the door. The night slipped out of the sky into her
neck; she felt the curtains; the room absorbed her
skin with the hopeless sky and the bluish light of
morning. She was afraid of her own breath as she
crept towards sleep.

Jacqueline woke with the clash of clattering buckets,
and asked the cause of her husband's accident. On
Williams's orders the files were sealed so her questions could not be answered. She was given a large
pile of reports – the relevant papers were mixed with
others to lose their meaning. Her urgent questions
were stopped by an anxious gesture of the doctor's
fat red hand.

Intermittently Jacqueline slipped her hand under the
warm bedclothes, dying to go downstairs, where the
windows were open and air blew in. Phillip's mouth
stiffened with sweat; she held him till he slept. Under
his pillow she found a cigarette; she looked at it faintly
in the light that leaked in through the curtains. Her
hand was trapped by his arm – it was not hers unless he
told her. Phillip lay shivering; she knew what her husband wanted, open and shut; opening herself brought
a smile as she kissed his eyes. She put her hand on his
mouth, rehearsed the cause of the accident, rubbed

hot coins against his legs. "Can't you tell me… how did it happen? Were you drunk?" "There's nothing to tell, ill as I am." The questions led home to his brother. Phillip refused to answer. Her hand rested on the counterpane; it was not important. She touched his cheek, and he promised to help, saying her name – Jacqueline – as though it had been water. She said he must pretend to be dazed. "Confuse them. That is the impression you need to make at the inquiry." She stroked his hair. "The lawyers will need your coopera-tion." "I must sleep." "There's the question of com-pensation. I have to live." "On my word of honour, there is no more I can say. I'll do what you wish, but put this bad boy straight back in his warm blankets as soon as you can." This was Phillip's pretence at being dazed, and it failed. "I'll leave for court tomorrow, if that is required. I saw Michael an hour ago. At the moment that the soul of your brother is real to you, leave him – not in your arms, but in a place of danger. Give others the burden of his life. When I'm through – it might be today – you can try to blame the guilty person." Phillip refused to name his brother, the cruel renegade, the hard kind. Michael thought he was safe; his younger brother had fallen. Phillip had to be moved, together with the equipment which preserved his life. The machine and the boy were taken to a room, his wife with him; he was bombarded slowly – there was plenty of time.

In the hospital there was nothing to do. "I've been after a job," Jacqueline said. "You've a job here, with me," Phillip pulled her hand – his reaction was to kiss – he persisted. "The interview is tomorrow; I'll leave

on the early train," she said. "Don't try to be smart,"
he said, sinking his teeth in. "I have my reasons – you'll
see – there'll be jobs for both of us – two new-comers.
You'll get on well." "I need you here. Everyone is being
moved into the corridor." "I am not afraid to leave you."
Phillip's hair, forehead and lips were quite strange.
Jacqueline felt drawn to men who looked sleek and
who wore boots. She smiled. "I have the job – I've been
accepted – there's no point in discussing it; there is
nothing more I can do here. I have seen your father – I
spent the whole day with him. Everything you need is
on the way." Phillip said: "All I ask is that we start off as
soon as possible. We'll say our goodbyes to the family,
go straight there. It won't be easy – it will require all
our energy and skill to get away, if you mean to take
me with you." "Your father doesn't want you to go."
Jacqueline said nothing about herself. "Talk it over –
persuade him to let me go. I'll be better off with you."
"It's no use, he won't let you go. It's late," she said.
"Trust me." "I waited for you – you didn't come – we
said Sunday the fifteenth of June." "Believe me, there's
no more to say; I must go alone this time." Phillip's face
had gone dark. "Go home and stay. I'll come." Tired
of the patternless walls in the middle of the afternoon,
the husband and wife could not find anything to say.

"Who's paying for this thing?" Phillip prodded the
bandage lying at his feet; he was in pain. The laser
aimed a beam of light to cut a millimetre deep – a
weapon from space to earth, the secret rescue squad,
the critical attempt. "The plan may be abandoned if
problems arise." The air held death lined up and waiting
for him; he saw no sense in delay. Phillip pulled back

his sleeve to look at his watch – he did it well, with confidence – his eyes on the other. His wife's mouth was an absent guest.

"Nothing but bad dreams." Whatever he was made of fell to pieces. He felt cold. The end of the life was the sound of yellow, rattling across the floor. Williams looked at the woman in the chair, her expression unchanged. Michael, in a coat, waited across the corridor, near the lavatory bowl, the dark nostril; he began to walk to reach the bowl; he looked down; his face lifted suddenly; he felt the weight of the dead, when time will not come. When Phillip died, his agony was equal to those fierce expressions flying over the surface of water, with a stroke in which neuter light and black were mixed in equal parts.

Phillip was pulled from the bed, his body opened and the parts numbered. It was impossible to make a mistake: it was efficient and peaceful. Two parts became one, then five, seven, ten together; the quantity of numbers grew – two hundred bones, three hundred muscles; the signs were placed on a chart; the mysterious blue in the red – a sign in the brain for hours.

Chapter 2

THE FACTORY MANAGEMENT undertook the funeral arrangements. Morale demanded that they be magnificent. Phillip's corpse would travel alone. If the multitude of mourners pressed too close, the coffin horses would presumably bolt. The family mourners followed the plumes. They were proud that death should be so popular. The purple drapes in the parks attracted crowds; mobs stood about in the streets to watch the ceremony in the cheerful place. The charming hats stalked the dignitaries who came for the kill; when it rained they slipped rapidly away. Williams mixed with the crowd; he talked to their children. It was an agonizing experience to attend the drama – the top hats hot and loudly ran from the rain and from the drums and other guns going off. The music and commentaries slid easily on; nothing had changed for the corpse; perhaps the coffin was carried a hundred feet or so from the cathedral; it was all very bizarre as the coffin crossed the circle: the lieutenant and the cortège fused; the candles died in hundreds; the crowds strained to view the sleek heads of the managers; the lucky ones watched from windows. It was like centuries ago; the men remained midgets and they trod the cathedral floor as the coffin cruised back and forth, and all were informed by radio about what was going on in the vast desert of stone. The skeletal saints combined with the choir around the altar, crosses of gold, heavy with thousands of forlorn candles. It was difficult to imagine when the first sadness began in the gun-metal gloom deposited year after year as the priestly voice intoned: "This man was outstanding in his field and a great loss to our work. Today the techniques and knowledge of conditions reduce the hazards of the past, but sometimes tragedy strikes and a new name is added to the roll of honour." Organ music porpoised from the Norman doors; squads of police created panic around them; it seemed that the fanfares with the gunfire had scared the police horses, and the crowd began to surge. Williams was safe in his car; cars had been reserved for the departmental managers, who took their wives and endured the long day; cars with black ribbons contained the widow and the rest of the mourning family; the desired result was achieved; the assembled boots and smells did not come over the radio; the guests strained forwards to the moderate feast – the ham and pork and German wine were flavoured in their imagination. Jacqueline fingered the family necklace as an onlooker climbed a lamp-post and focused his camera, slipped, hung by the strap, cheering the last of the uniforms. Men sold matches and apologized for doing so; acrobats swept the streets; soldiers wore their medals and stars. Williams had the uneasy feeling that he was not looking his best, as he waddled away to the beginning of the home-bound procession. The father of the dead boy had arrived and had to return; he was committed by the one to the other. Williams poised at the top of the high steps, ready to dive into the crowd; an arrow from a cliff shot into the incomprehensible sea, ready to take part in the mass celebration that was basically meaningless, yet it was impossible not to be moved by the sight and size of the idiot crowd. Michael's beard battled and leapt to be seen before he fell back, wedged against Jacqueline; she slipped away; a flare of white thigh, a glacier surrounded by feathers, her skirt soiled and black; Michael followed; he was as fast. The great battalions marched the route commemorating the military and terrible death; the bearded boy surfaced brilliantly, his hand on the curve, then Jacqueline knifed through the sweat-filled crowd, lost in the depths by twisting quicker than the little stubborn maniac in love with the shrimp he chased; she heard him cry as, exhausted, he clambered away, and Williams came up, saying "I'm a man – can I help?" as Michael returned and moved with the procession; encumbered by three parcels, the wooden troops stood still; the lines of diplomatic penguins froze. Michael said "I live close by", disentangled himself from the column, scrambled back for his coat, preserved for a century in cathedral stone; he dug it out in the manner of an archaeologist, emerged a clad and decent man – a formal male.

Phillip's body was buried – it turned to earth. In the end he could not omit his bones from the new experience. He lost his appetites, he had no further interest in science, in new ideas or violent action; he was incapable of the sudden jerk into responsiveness; he was dead to the act of love.

Michael sat for an hour over a cup of coffee. "It's like a war and he's lost." A girl in high-heeled shoes offered a cigarette in passing. He did not blame her, but she was too fat; he went to an amusement arcade to pass the time.

On his way home Williams passed a wall. He was silent. He watched a boy sink into the earth; a man stamped his foot. He would find the windows of his home hidden by curtains. Williams opened the door of Jacqueline's room; the woman had not heard him. He had a view of her face. She was his son Phillip's wife – he remembered the picture. Williams went in, and she offered him food. He went for a walk in the park for lack of anywhere else to go. His son was dead, but the widow was alive and Williams was afraid she would make trouble. The park was no man's land – he was on his own, thinking. Williams's father had been a war hero; the monument to the fallen still bore his name; his father had been an engineer and a good man; Williams had been the eldest child, ugly and subdued; his parents had not known what to make of him. As the eldest son he had joined the firm; the second son had stayed at home; the third would have been a doctor. It was his parents' dream. Williams's father had devoted himself to the education of his son – he had given him books to read; his eyes became nervous; his forehead marked with misery. In this park Williams's own boys had played under the ash tree; the game had depended on the number of boys – three, five, or seven – the lot of them chasing butterflies under the ash tree, and their colours were the same as those on the holy medallions with symbols and ornaments in the form of men and animals. An egg had been found by Phillip: first a white one – their value was small – then a speckled. The blue had been incomparable. The boys had kept green sticks, which had flourished throughout winter, throwing flowers from leafless stalks in old age. No further mistake would occur if he fixed his mind on the green.

Chapter 3

T HERE WAS A SOMEWHAT austere reaction in Williams's home to anything that disturbed the routine. He was a man in a suit with heavy eyes and fingers waiting for breakfast. He was sorry about the death – his friends knew why – there had been too much delay; Williams had had a good night's sleep; he doubted if the inquest were desirable; the difficulty would be in dealing with questions; there were those who died – his son, himself too; no point in fighting the custom; we all had our customs; they were hygienic; there was no necessity for an inquiry, but in the event he would do what he could. Williams had not been given the cooperation he was entitled to, but he completed his complicated arrangements. He had to change his suit; he had agreed to attend the inquest; his head down before the open window, his teeth chattering.

The inquest was to be conducted by one of those institutions under managerial control and meticulous supervision staffed exclusively by lawyers. The two judges resembled each other, and all lawyers resembled them; they were dressed alike, without charm: no love on their faces, which showed two black curves on the head, imitation eyebrows, a nose and lips – apparently a face, which could be studied, the neck of each different when examined closely. One found differences in the wigs, which curved backwards and were arranged between the ears; the artificial hair passed under a comb and appeared as string. A number of long pins served to secure the hair (some of the pins snatching at fresh air), could be removed and the hair tied with a ribbon. No name was understood. To mention a name was to cause uneasy smiles. The lawyers made no errors as to dress, wore black gowns and white cravats, the badges of their profession. "In a strange country, be prepared for surprises," they would say; if they found a colleague taking the first meal of the day without wig and gown, they would call him mad. "And the gown should lap from left to right, not from right to left, or there is no equity." The right wing of the judges' gowns overlapped and left and almost completely covered it, except for the hidden fold which encased the flank. The reverse arrangement was adopted by junior lawyers and their clerks. The judges were invariably right-handed, the others left-handed. To know the one was to know the other. As for justice, they understood well enough how that should be arranged.

"Certainly not!" Williams dealt with their preliminary questions. They knew or would know everything. There had been no delay in treating the unfortunate person, no suspicion of unpunctuality. "Sauce!" he said, as his ill-adjusted magnificence sat himself down as if to dinner. "Unpunctual? Never. We eat at seven. To the dot. With my work it is the same. I arrive at eight. And at eight I begin."

The presiding judge had some doubts as to which of the lawyers should be recognized as the deceased's accredited representative. While each of the five lawyers addressed the court, Williams's attitude was one of injured pride. He doodled on blotting paper, fiercely scribbling semicircles as if he had given a lifetime to their study.

The poisonous face of the widow was in the court. Jacqueline took the oath; she spoke perfectly – a flute learning the alphabet, no letter forgotten. The senior judge was unfriendly, his eyes unhappy as he glanced at her. The court was cold; it believed in reason.

"He was my husband. He died alone. I went for a walk. I did not know it would happen." Jacqueline wanted to know why he had died. It was the doctor's fault – people did not call in the doctor to die, but to be cured. She had been shopping when the news came; she had bought a thin linen dress suitable for the spring; they had been married at Easter, but the day his coffin was driven to church it had rained. She apologized: "It's nothing", blinking in the smoke-filled room; dangerous fatigue in the narrow face; trying for most of the day, for four or five hours, to remember what had happened; there was little to remember; the weather had been fine. "On the eighth day Mr Williams came to see me and wished to tell me something. I met him in my room, and he spoke to me again, but I did not understand. I thought he was lying." "Then what do you claim you did?" "I was going to see my husband when I came home from work. I said goodnight and went upstairs. When I returned on Tuesday evening, they told me about him being dead. I went into the room and put on the lights; Phillip appeared dead – he was lying on his side; that is all I know." "Did you notice any blood?" "There was blood on his shirt." "There is not a scrap of evidence that he was wearing a shirt." "There was no fire in the room. He had his woollen pyjamas over his shirt – he needed the warmth. I can't remember more.

The floor was uneven, it was dangerous; the boards were noisy when I carried the body to the bed. I don't remember more." "You said you saw blood on the shirt. Was that true?" "No, not true. My memory was bad. The lie was about the shirt. It was his pyjama jacket over his shirt." The false statement about the shirt took several minutes to sort out. Jacqueline said she understood that someone had panicked when he applied the tourniquet a second time, and she looked at him. Williams traced thoughts in her eyes; they were triangles; not pure – there was a hint of shame; and abruptly he withdrew to the farthest corner of the table, away from his son. "You persist in allegations against a perfectly innocent man?" She answered no. "My learned friend reminds me… I will tell you what is in my mind: your husband is the victim – you are his wife – along you come and say whatever is most profitable – you carry it further, tell a dozen lies, begin lying about a shirt; you cannot extricate yourself – lies are added to lies; you end by admitting you tore the shirt with your hands." "What is the question?" "Answer the question." "The answer is yes." She might have answered him, but he had reached the end of his cross-examination, more or less, and he sat down. "No further questions, thank you." The woman held her handbag: "He was all I had, my lord."

A splendid oak beam supported the circular roof, the bench of green chairs; the senior judge sat alone on the central chair; behind the chair was an arch, the coat of arms, the sword, benches for students, seats for distinguished spectators, incomparable libraries, a box, a jail. The octagonal ceiling surmounted the glass-wood frame; the place was an exception; it measured the rare occasion – it may have done so ten or twenty times.

Guarded, Michael went to the box; his face matched his careful hair; the elder brother took the book and swore to God, and his life depended on it. The professional man with years to live: he took his degree, the son of a celebrated man. The lawyers rose and charged and pleaded and sat. Michael was required to speak in detail, and he complied. The court was concerned with the brothers and with the wife – they were regarded as one – was it impossible to separate the brothers or the man from his wife? Michael answered yes. To separate even the days was hopeless; he picked his words, determined to exonerate himself. He came near to the truth; the evidence emerged, then he almost lost by trying. There was a gap of two hours – he could not explain it. Yet this is not to say, "This is the man who got on badly; this is the one who lied." He went through that day. He was brought to court, where he confessed himself. His was an expert art. He would be impossible to answer. The one who might have helped was not called. Asked about the accident, Michael told God the truth and gave minute thought to the effect. The lawyers demanded it: they demanded justice. The trouble was the wife. Her suspicions could not be hushed up. Michael described the circumstances. "I am sure you will be most careful," his lawyer said, when he mentioned the blood on the wheel; though the two acts were part of one, done by a man in a state of mind, they were regarded as one, impossible to separate. When questioned about the transfusions, Michael said he had not noticed the label on the bottle, and then the young man's voice altered – it was noted the way it changed. "His voice tends to fall." "I have a quiet voice – it is the result of the war, my lord," Michael explained. It was nothing of the kind. Yet the man had lost his voice. They knew nothing of his life, but the judges were waiting. "Will you take a glass of water?" "It doesn't matter – I can manage." A decent sort. "And you go to your father and confess and follow it up with a speech about what you are alleged to have found, yet you knew perfectly well that Mr Williams was in no ways involved?" "Yes." Had he made a statement? He had done that too. Yes. Hour after hour. Wisely he stuck to what he knew. "I had to live." It sounded sweet. He said he was tired. He was nothing of the kind.

The judges retired to consider their verdict. The two drank the thin white wine; the green and tasty stomachs stood on the polished table; their wigs and hats on the convenient shelf; each day a brandy in a balloon. And to follow? They pushed their stomachs close; each had a slit for dropping in pieces of pie, each a toothpick in a pocket; they picked their teeth and drew blood; it took ten minutes. The judge's clerk, a clean and handsome man, said the veal was good. It was blind white bread from the slaughter-house; meat in frozen form. The tribunal announced: "The only comment we can make is that he killed himself by smashing his head repeatedly against a wall."

As he left the court, Williams murmured to his son, "It was your last blunder." Michael pulled back his sleeve to look at his watch; he did it well, with confidence, his eyes on the other. "Never mind – nothing but bad dreams." Michael walked away from the man in the black suit, remembered something and turned. "I don't know – it was not too bad. I thought she might bring up the question of compensation." He caught sight of the widow across the room; she shyly recognized him, walked up to him; Michael shook hands, said "I'll be back in a minute" and hurried away.

Chapter 4

WORKING WITH THE TWO OTHERS, in a closed
room, Williams was led away by the world of
astrology and knockabout spiritualism. Spanning two
wings of tragedy, brother and widow, he postponed his
final condition – their support was seen by his friends;
he was judged a success, yet an abyss divided him from
them. The last moments recurred – the spiral of ideas
which stood for time – as if he had died at the same
time. Michael and Jacqueline were a constant relief;
being young, it was they who catalysed the revelation.
Worship of life was proclaimed – that which commenced
and closed, proceeded, reiterated its appeal. Williams's
apocalyptic visions were cries of hope in a form which
contained his age. The man of humanity was approach-
ing, he was coming; belief was imminent – they would
be believers among themselves in the rigmarole of faith.
Williams had a new birth at sixty-eight; he declared
he heralded new ideas; they would appear to him in
a room very similar to this, with startling and precise
details. When he felt the storm preceding the advent,
Williams walked rapidly from West to East, declared
the date of the clouds; clothed in glory, he would reveal
his ideas, surrounded by his sons – they would sit on

thrones; the thing he most anxiously awaited was that the judges would reappear; he constantly awaited their judgement; he would be caught off his guard, as in the times of Noah, and judged according to his deeds. Ready for sentence, as the elder, Williams kept watch; he prepared for the day when he would come to the feast like a thief in the night, and run from one end of the crowded hall to the other, making declarations of friendship with all.

Sprawled on the couch, pretending to read important documents, Michael listened to his father on the telephone for half an hour, lying opposite, feet against the wall, hands in pockets, legs stretched out, periodically contradicting some assertion of the speaker, ridiculing his virtues, bored, almost ill; Michael appeared to be listening carefully, but the young widow by his desk was his primary interest. It was Jacqueline's first visit to the burly man on the top floor of the building; Williams had not avoided her – he had made himself accessible; he had nothing to hide. Michael had warned her that she would find his father charming; he would pour tea; they would drink great quantities; he would discuss her problems and say, "You will find out one day, my dear, it is not easy to deal with colleagues."

Michael glanced warily at his father before walking over to Jacqueline; he sat on the edge of the desk, played with an India rubber. The two men were on their feet as tea was brought in, and Michael was in his corner making himself obscure, checking figures connected with the payment of staff – he concentrated steadily, stood by the girl; Williams inserted himself between them, taller by inches, with greater dignity. The younger man tried to copy the expression and style of the older, but could not manage the eyebrows. Jacqueline flicked the rubber to the floor; Michael was expected to retrieve it – he knelt, looked up at her; Williams's forehead frowned in protest – he had recently started frowning – this nervous twitching was unprecedented; it intensified until the face reddened, but it did not affect his position. Jacqueline anxiously motioned the son to sit down, and he obeyed. Each glance indicated mutual observation; the quarrel had grown quiet, but any chance of compromise – avoiding a scene, taking no risks and getting into bed and sleeping quietly – were barred. Williams studied the list of men to be sacked, but did not see his son's name. The dazzling white of murder steamed into his mind, the strap on his wrist; his coat was soft; he had stepped into the rain with the wind blowing, a hat on the grey hair. Williams heard the insolent voice, passed over it twice, his concentration interrupted by laughter; Michael's face would tell him nothing; the sniggering stopped. Michael explained that the inquiry would have to be reopened – an arrangement which corresponded perfectly with the requirements of the situation; in future the firm would not be troubled by claims for workmen's compensation; widows' benefits would figure in company policy and "thank Heaven for it, if one may make so bold". Williams's answer to these proposals was clear (he put his hand to his spectacles): "Some form of legal affidavit will normally be required, on the simple condition… that, in a case like this, would not be unreasonable, though it might be disagreeable for those concerned. My dear Michael, you fail to understand, the uncertainty will make matters worse, in so far as... Everyone has noticed that... the most acceptable solution..." Williams was beginning to sound as if his mouth would remain open until it was time for him to die. "The question of whether the idea has got about that the stage has been reached at which the question would become other than academic..." "What's that he's saying?" Jacqueline whispered to Michael. "Are you sufficiently aware of your own position?" Williams continued: "I suppose you realize that not one of those fellows had my permission—" "—To be a nuisance?" Not that it worried Williams unduly, he remembered now the affair was well in hand: he had seen the certificate – the widow had signed – the other documents would be in his hands within the week. He had yet to produce a first-hand witness to the accident, but he was not obliged to do so. "If I had your nostrils, Michael, I would smell him out." Williams was a poet who found excitement in realizing he could do anything. "The lawyers have investigated the position – the books can be verified; any irregularities occurred long ago; if they did find anyone who took part in the so-called conspiracy, it would be too late now to reopen the matter." "Don't worry – that conclusion is fairly obvious." Michael's tone was routine; it was not intended to be reassuring. Though he lacked that period of undisturbed contemplation necessary before taking a final decision, Williams knew that when they searched his desk they would find old newspapers and leaves of vegetables and scraps of blanket, and it would be for them to insinuate their relevance...

The interminable feud continued. The worm of guilt produced a stifled silence. Short of breath and of time, as if his life had been in danger, Williams went towards the door. There was too much light coming through the windows; he stood in the middle of the room; the sunlight hit him like the beam of an arc lamp. "I humbly apologize for my little joke, my dear." Passing Jacqueline, he felt her breasts brush against his arm. "I appreciate your point of view," she said coldly. Williams would have the pleasure of seeing her again. He crossed the room, lit a cigarette and talked of business affairs. She sucked her finger with unconcern. Williams moved, without faltering, his shoes in the pile carpet; the flow of their common sentences joined in understanding. "Am I a bad boy?" She had her hand in front of her mouth as she shut the door. "I am sorry if I made a mistake," she said. "It will have to be corrected." Her black dress had gone violet; the mourning had ended. "You have been kind to me," she said. "What's that?" Jacqueline's sharp nails searched for a match. Williams handed her his lighter. "Quite wonderful," she said. "Well, I don't know." Williams considered the course of events; he had discharged his duty; he was curious to know if she were living alone. Worried by the delay in payment of her compensation, Jacqueline asked how she was meant to pay the rent. "I'm afraid I'm not exactly sure where the petty cash is kept," he said, "and you know that cheques must be countersigned by a fellow director." "I understand."

Williams showed no surprise when Jacqueline applied for a job as his secretary. She was concerned to know what the wages were, the training she would be given. "You will be taken care of, with cheaper lunches in the canteen than you can find outside." She would have to be vetted for her tact in shutting doors and her shining religious convictions. Fortunately she had been seen coming out of chapel, and her references contained the necessary information. It could have been worse: she might have been less attractive. Women did not have the same feelings as men – they were equally insufferable, with their childish faith and hatreds. Williams could not put up with it any longer – he was a "man of culture", an "individual in a hostile world".

With Jacqueline, Williams visited the men's quarters and questioned them about their work: "How do you spend your time?" "We spend out time working, naturally." "Have you any complaints?" "Our main difficulty is in getting backwards and forwards to work, but we manage." The men helped each other cheerfully when the sun shone, and concentrated on evading the innumerable regulations. Williams had ordered that no variation in working conditions be permitted – the windows were to remain shut in winter and summer, except for a period of six minutes at noon of each day. At first the men found it a little difficult to acclimatize themselves to the new routine, but soon it became a pleasant thing for them to look forward to the noon and the entry into their rooms of what looked like breath. Sexual satisfaction was as far away as the moon, and the moon was always high. Their notion of the idea of a woman was that she would come in a plane "out of the cloudless sky", and they would recognize her at a glance, though she would tend to relate the whole experience to the everyday life of a normal person. If there were a female visitor, the men would pick her up – children, dogs and all – and carry her into the main workshop. They would call it the miraculous visitation, and think of it in terms of the mental strain in the isolated place. Most of the men were satisfied by a few pin-ups on the walls – a red-haired naked girl swimming in the sea, a figure of a blonde languidly reclining with seashells and sunbursts, dark girls half asleep against crescent moons with ragged drapery caught (inevitably) by the wind, an amusing dragonfly in purple, white and puce, a woman in an ornamental garden feeding peacocks, a naked girl embracing a bull between pillars, a real girl with real rain shining on her yellow plastic mac, the form of an American dancer called Loie Fuller, whipping up the train of her dress into a billowing hood, and beneath the billows was concealed a light bulb advertising the fame of the Folies Bergère. In their cramped dormitories lit only by a Primus, they lived like dogs without yelping. Their remoteness became less noticeable, except for a certain giantism, as they crouched over their cooking stoves forty or fifty feet high. "It is good business to watch over the welfare of employees – they work harder," Williams said. The men fed like starving dogs in their eagerness to be away; they were harnessed to their work; they experienced a more intense loathing for the factory than for any other point on earth. "Each man has a set target

– a comfortable day's work. If you work harder the bonus increases. To a large extent it's up to you." The unskilled workers were transferred from place to place like units of frozen meat. When each man was at his accustomed place, painting the girders, or repairing the massive concrete huts, all thinking of women – the same sort of women – when the work was done and they had assembled the machines, produced two thousand one hundred and ninety units per day, the atmosphere became gay, everybody talking to his neighbour; they drove off at speed across the countryside, stocked with tons of food and fuel, with the intention of travelling hundreds of miles without pause, knowing that at any time they could be picked up – precisely and securely removed back to their place of work, and anchored there so that they could not move.

"And now?" Jacqueline asked. "Now you will settle down and find suitable friends. No pressure will be brought to bear on you – the unhappy past will be forgotten," Williams said. An official statement had been issued, but the smell would not disappear – not that anyone was to blame: the problem had been inherited; the case had been handled beautifully, but rumours that facts had been suppressed were too widespread to be contained. Michael had been no help. "These young chaps, I'd have fired them like that – slapdash, no respect, feeble, don't give a damn." "Michael has taken to wearing a bow tie," Jacqueline said. "He puts his arm round me and calls me darling. He's joined the golf club." Phillip had had such long curly hair, remarkable hair; he had played the piano – he was marvellous. Williams said he would have a talk with his son, but not for several days. Jacqueline had come prepared with the draft Williams had asked her to type, with red-ink decorations under the word, as the singular was corrected to the plural. "There's an odd paragraph here; I don't understand it at all." She looked annoyed. Williams said she should not pay too much attention to his corrections – suggestions – it was merely an informal report, a preliminary to action. "Know what that means?" The arc of her eyebrows framed her reply. Williams asked her if she knew Michael well. She said he was "rather boyish, desperately provincial, though always very sweet to me, especially when he plays his practical jokes". "Are you fond of him?" "I find him interesting." Michael overheard this tribute, as he raised again the men's demands that the inquiry be reconvened. "Do you not share their concern at the possibility of further similar accidents?" "No one's really thought about where this agitation can lead. We've not heard yet from those directly involved," Williams said. "Some of the machinery is dangerous." "If it is dangerous, of course it has a guard round it. Our workers wear protective clothing, including rubber overshoes. They are not allowed to eat sweets; they may not sleep at the bench; they are forbidden to set the building on fire. Their names are included on the roll of honour. If there's a war, they're busy with that," Williams said. "We play for time while the men become impatient," Michael said; generally speaking there was no order – irregularities continued – something on more military lines was required. When he was warned that he could be replaced "by someone a little older, more mature",

Michael said the board must decide – only they could dismiss him – but he had reason to believe that they were not out of sympathy with progressive views.

Williams intended to avoid any dispute with his son; he sent him as his deputy to key meetings and inquests. "They say I am prejudicing my position, but I have no intention of doing so. If there is a conflict, those who remain loyal will gain and deserve my support. Confidence is a weapon. My word goes while I am in command."

It was not yet September; preparations for winter had not begun. An excited yapping and barking and shouting was heard from the stores. Williams investigated immediately, but could find nothing – no animal was unearthed, no woman discovered. From then on every incoming and outgoing vehicle was checked thoroughly. On Sunday evenings, when the men invariably tumbled out of their cars, drunk and exhausted, they were taken to the medical wing and meticulously examined. They were given weights to carry the equivalent of enormous distances, and the question posed: "What keeps them going? Why do they have no desire to return to civilization?" Their skin was microscopically examined for boils, and particular attention was paid to the smallest protuberance above the surface of the skin. It appeared to the doctors that certain men benefited from exertion – those with the weakest constitutions – and they were made to wear special overalls made from non-porous plastic, as thick as a normal overcoat but infinitely hotter.

Williams continued his superficial but gracious tour of inspection. For an hour he timed the builders' labourers slinging bricks. Presently he saw his name chalked on a wall, the letters over eleven feet high, the edges deeply chiselled out along the sides. The offensive slogan could be seen from his office window; he asked Michael to investigate, but his son ignored him. Williams could not find the right words, the right approach, when he spoke to the men. The best workers remained slumped on the ground; the cackling high spirits of the others offended him. But these men were useful – they would not have been employed otherwise. Their wild habits were tolerated, though they made the site a jungle at night. In one place, two or three times a night there would be a fight; they did not hide it – they announced the fact. The victim could be recognized from the running and shouting; when one shouted the others joined in; their purpose was to announce the existence of one individual to another. Williams walked as far from them as he could, heard his telephone ring and raced back to his office. "It's all right," Jacqueline said; "Michael has dealt with it."

Williams worked late that night; the building was in darkness except for his office. Jacqueline normally went home at six, but she waited with him. Williams called her his confidential secretary. A secretary? Behind the name was a woman. He found this touching. She wished to be found attractive. She patted the hands of the old man who waited for her; he showed his teeth and gums, his arms out to embrace; he pinned her close in her chair, his lips tight against her blouse; she put an arm around his shoulders and enjoyed the desire and embarrassment moving in the recesses of the old man's body. Then she looked at his watch and said it was time for her to go.

Williams stood against the wall, a man watching the night; he heard nothing. He waited until three in the morning, staring at the wall opposite. He knew that the responsibility for keeping intruders away was not his – it was in good hands – yet he kept watch until he fell asleep. He was woken by a tapping on the side of his head. The person must have the key to the office – the door was open. Williams turned off the lights – no sign of anyone – a man's form behind the curtains; the shape might have been a shadow. He crossed to the window in a businesslike way; the two were separated by a shadow; the man held a spanner. The high wall was impossible to climb. The intruder held a spanner level with his head; the room gleamed with the varnished surfaces of desk and chairs – soft glowing on sheets of paper, the rest dark. Standing still, the man adjusted his mask; the face remained hidden. Williams knew who it was – he was certain. He would deal with this himself – he would not want it to get about. It was probably someone with permission to enter the building at odd times, perhaps to clean, or check for security. His senses caught the sounds of the night; he had not yet made up his mind – there was something he could not account for; when daylight came he would investigate thoroughly. He was stopped by a patch of damp on the carpet – a rumpling of the pile, as if somebody had lain there. Williams was no fool – he knew what that meant: a person had passed close enough to touch, yet he had not seen him. He experienced the fear of one who knows he has only just escaped.

When Williams left the building in the dawn light, five men stood where they could not be seen, below the half-completed stairs. An obstruction on the stairs was held by a piece of rope – a cunning move. These men were unknown; Williams had seen only one of them before. A man stepped close; a hand climbed and crept over the soft clothes and held his mouth. The hand was removed from the mouth, a man struck him; one laughed, one whistled, one gripped his head and told him to behave himself. One spoke a warning and forced him to the ground. The act of sudden violence when it came. This thug knew the texture of a truncheon. The blow must be directed upwards, with force to meet force. A dictatorial note: "Get out of my way." There was no way of saying thank you. This specimen should be isolated, for psychological and physical reasons. Note the shape of the back, the height of the head. The blow on the left side of the jaw. Effect of judicial hanging. Instantaneous. A jarring motion was abruptly and very rapidly repeated through the limited space. The design of the body had one function only: the crack on the jaw. Sticking plaster was used as a gag and to secure the wrists to the leg of the table. A nose was picked before the application of the plaster. A person under the influence of fear shivers, as the flesh under the surgeon's knife – though more fundamental and enduring. Contortions in the face, like a fit. Drowning. Keep on, keep on. Pronounced dead. Throw him back. He would not cry for help. He began to judge the time, to get on top of it. Williams did not ask what had happened; he strained to hear their talk. "I was fixed on this job at the start. Once

I make a start I like a tremendous amount of thinking before I start." A sheet of newspaper on the floor divided Williams from his attackers; a photograph from the jungle war helped to calm him. "I was always keen on animals, especially leopards." "Time has run out." Williams knew how to fight: if attacked, hold height. He stayed on the floor until they had gone, the newspaper in fragments.

There had been no disturbance, and the shadows collapsed across the lawn, the flower beds, the ground beyond the factory. Five men vaulted a low fence, merged with the unimportant surface and the hard marks of darkness.

Chapter 5

WILLIAMS COULD NOT REACH the house in which to fall; his eyes hurt through the darkness towards home. Some came and carried him, searched and found sticks and fingerprints. The place was like an air raid with smashed machines on the pavement, iron shapes of every kind. Here was his strength; in his suit he returned to the place where the men had broken in. His friends restrained him – his back against the breach in the wall. Williams crawled over to meet those who were travelling east, and found a body across a gate, lying flat. The electrified fencing was reinforced, traffic halted; there were no expresses – speed was a rarity, a ray of the past – as guards checked countless strangers until they disappeared, cluttered with luggage and fears. The young men travelled to work in the form of an arrow flashing in phase; they came in cars and often with hope; they worked in groups, while the aged were pushed in flat trucks with machinery and equipment open to the weather. At the congested turning, Williams saw life sometimes at the end of the street, scrutinizing the eastbound lorries – the intruders might come again from there. He crossed the park, intent on discovering the link between his crime and theirs, climbing every day more fences as he found them; he studied the ergonomic solution under crash conditions, the work done by unit force on a body which moved in the direction of the action of the force.

The morning broke across the workshop with the warmth of an engine. A new person, a different man, Williams ventured into the main assembly room to supervise the mechanics testing a new machine. Two men stared down at the coils of copper – one shook his head, fiddled in the dust with his boot, their faces lit from below by the light from their inspection lamps. Williams walked backwards and forwards, clinking coins in his pocket. The dynamo alone, though incomplete, was bigger than a tank; it came near to scraping the galvanized roof. Williams seemed to have forgotten the previous night; he enjoyed the tension – his eyes joined, he looked fixedly at their feet, working on a plan like a watch, caressing the polished chrome. He had returned to his rightful function; he advanced on his own. In front of these men Williams's face developed, reached perfection; his mind became specialized, the lines on his face travelled predetermined tracks, said things he would have preferred to hide. He would have sacrificed his right arm, the stump casually dipped in creosote. He wondered whether the oil was properly lubricating the soft bed of brass.

On Sunday Williams walked down to the empty workshop wearing a pair of old tennis shoes. It was difficult to know what to make of him, staring down at the still machine, holding one of his two teddy-bear mascots. By the light of the weekend emergency lamps he plugged the cable into position, fixed the wires onto the switching block and carefully checked the criss-crossed multi-coloured electrical connections. A globe revolved; there were three in a row. The dominant eyes became less assertive. Williams enjoyed the theories as to how and when his power would end – everyone knew it, but he intended the lonely role to continue for years, flashing messages to unseen people across the world, turning his back on those he wished to avoid.

With a few friends Michael sat in a room thick with smoke, beginning a movement which would have been successful if the old man had allowed it to get under way. Their conversations had hardly started when the inherent danger of factions was pointed out. They suspended discussion until the formal company meeting opened; while they waited they ate fruit.

Williams hurriedly presented his new plan: an elaboration and specialization of previous plans, it transposed all departments of given size into bodies of a higher type; each would acquire a new structure and function. The organization was an organism composed of cells; each fulfilled a distinct function. "Some will be concerned with the outer fabric of the building, some with work discipline, others with safety, the rest with administration; in no case will an inferior department be permitted to function as efficiently as its superior. Those responsible for outer coverings will defer to those producing complex surfaces, who will in turn be supervised by appropriate functionaries." It was due to his profound understanding of the wider context of the theory of organization that Williams achieved success.

Flexibility was his characteristic; while his colleagues hardened with age, Williams retained contact with unorthodox methods, allowed himself to be infiltrated by new ideas – thus he retained overall control without question and without difficulty. Michael termed the new plan "a tribute to ingenuity and extraordinary resilience". But Williams had got into his stride. He recalled that it was he who had developed the process by which tokens were accepted as money. "I asked all my employees, on my birthday, to bring me their wages in exchange for tokens. I would reward them for their long and hazardous lives. I acquired the capital to buy machinery, became a director, and ceased to live among the poor. I was enterprising and spent long hours improving my original process; a good head – I knew the value of my own invention; I liked it, I tried it, I had good fortune. The first factory was built by the river, where the vessels came from the north. They came to me for a design that had strength: I showed them the frame; I eliminated dangerous bends and projections. Harness in front, unconscious analysis behind. The single stroke from door to floor. I placed a mirror to satisfy the vanity – the image was upside down, corrected by a suitable lens. I would not have my customers moved sharply; I protected them like eggs; I strapped them in against flexible shelves that folded upwards. In their view, in the window, the display was always lit, always visible. I took care that they remembered my name. I invited them to come to me; I kept them by force. Till now I have not been concerned with prestige. I have moved over the world uncared for, searching out new methods and markets, sleeping in trains, seeking the most modern, the ultra-progressive. I received an historic award, which I disregarded – it had no relevance to my work. And still the telephone rings around the world!" The last words were lost in the scrape of chairs as Michael indicated that it was time for the luncheon adjournment.

Lunch lasted two hours; it did not matter what was eaten. A speech was made; it did not matter what was said. A decoration was hung round the neck of a guest, a necklace round the neck of a girl. A speech was read from a sheet of paper; the speaker drank cold water; he was a government official; he scratched his head and wasted time; he spoke vaguely; he had "come to learn"; Williams did not hear a word; his eyes concealed his thoughts; the brief applause ended in silence. Williams spoke shortly: "My business is the world; I am a company director; I retain my convictions; all are welcome; I even employ the man who killed my son – it is all the same to me." He held his cup of coffee; the saucer sloped; it was small and white. Michael watched his father pick it up – with palms open, Williams shook the saucer to demonstrate the hold; feeling its lower surface he rolled it sideways. As he leant forwards, the chair legs shifted under him; he tilted sharply; his feet pressed to the crossbar; he lost his balance, grabbed his son's shoulders before he crashed with the chair to the floor. Michael helped him up. Williams began to hum a tune; he had succeeded in becoming a millionaire; he would cheat them in the end. At the mention of Jacqueline's name, the stormy and aggressive man was diverted by his own thoughts. Michael said she was proving invaluable; she was a trained nurse as well as the perfect secretary.

"We need a stenographer to take the minutes—" "I'm busy. Don't interrupt." Michael waited till the mood passed – he knew his father's mind. Williams studied his official portrait on the wall; the sense of disturbance made the features incomprehensible; he tapped his fingernail impatiently against the heavy gilt frame; his thoughts poured grey tape through a wind machine – little scrabblings, symptoms of restlessness. "Can't lounge around like this." Michael turned abruptly. "I said – someone—" Williams opened the window behind him, nodded twice as his son spoke, beat twice with his hand, walked across the room, returned and stood listening to the rain by the open window raining eighteen inches away and tentatively spilling from the gutter to the car park below. Michael closed the window. He wore a youthful smile above the unlit passage and into the collar; his face took on a tanned healthy look from the crowded furniture; he appeared as cool as before lunch, except that the eyes were watchful. "Watcher, soldier," Michael joked, handing over the slips of paper, or money. Williams received them slowly, looked angry. "Lunch is over – have to get back now, understand?" the father said sullenly from his chair. "And don't forget to take your umbrella along." Michael put on his raincoat, buttons on the shoulders; he hovered in front of the old man. "Did you wish to see me?" he asked. Williams turned away from him. Michael came forwards and went past, saying "Shall I lead the way?" to Jacqueline, as she slipped by, trying not to be seen. She was wearing a man's shirt and trousers, which Williams appeared to find amusing. "I still feel an attraction for any passing woman that comes along; I should be past all that nonsense now, but just the other day—" "You make him nervous," Michael said to Jacqueline; he held her hand as they walked from the room.

One curl of the match occupied the room, lit his throat, his match with the cigarette close, and on that the cigarette stuck. Williams gave the waitress half a crown and placed his cup on the table. He was absorbed by it; the smoke in silence slipped to his shoulder. A passing touch jogged the table on which he was writing. In the yard below a car drowned itself in the empty cup.

When the meeting resumed, for two hours Williams's voice made the room vibrate. "How do you feel?" He did not know what was wrong. "When it comes to the point at which we can decide the manner in which we can achieve the object in view, it became apparent that it cannot be perpetrated in the manner intended. We cannot do as we wish. That may seem a fundamental objection…" He rested a moment, recovered, coughed, turned a stream of phlegm over his suit. "I propose… I apologize."

"Maybe," drawled Michael, fingering his clean shirt, studying the agenda. "We might now turn to the next item. I am pleased to be able to inform you, gentlemen, that the turnover for the first four months of the current financial year has increased by practically the total increase in turnover for the whole of the last year. We shall repeat our interim dividend at seven and a half per cent, and promise a second interim payment before the end of March. It is not practicable at this stage to forecast the amount, but coupled with the fall in profit from £1.06 millions to £816,000 in the first half of the current year, the prospect is not inspiring. The Company has problems – sales at home have fallen; the outlook is uncertain in spite of recent improvement. Exceptional rain has affected production, but the backlog should be made up in the latter part of the year. Sales and profits from July to December should exceed those for the first half of the year, suggesting a total before tax of over £1.6 millions against last year's total of £2.1 millions." Michael was loudly cheered when he concluded: "If it is said we have to pay the price for efficiency in organization, then I say we have paid that price and we are not going to pay more. We have suffered enough." Michael added that the new plan sounded "marvellous and very intricate, but we need to know the facts, not merely an idea without details".

Williams got to his feet and said, "We have a plan, but we can only know the beginning; the end no man can know – we must accept that. We will retain the same two thousand men, three thousand machines, but new buildings and new management. I will intensify my study of organization. My mind has been working on problems of past and place – each connected with the plan and integrated with the overall scheme. My son is ignorant of the elementary truths I have tried to teach him; he thinks a skilled worker is indifferent, indistinguishable from a machine – one among ten million. But he will learn that from a lifetime's study a pattern appears: man resembles the ape, but the human form emerges and closes the series; man is an animal – nothing more wonderful."

Michael proposed a committee to explore the problem. "But meanwhile we might do something about these chairs. For too long we have suffered considerable discomfort on account of the boardroom chairs and the generally poor standard of seating at these meetings. I for one do not intend to tolerate discomfort. We shall rise for a period each morning and each afternoon. The chairman's throne is upholstered in leather, but I dare say even he is feeling the strain."

The telephone rang. Williams held the receiver awkwardly. It took him an hour to complete a sentence – he stopped several times; Michael looked at his watch. Williams continued slowly to make the words fit his face.

With the meeting adjourned, Jacqueline remained a familiar point in the room. Williams turned to her – her simplicity pleased him. She was replacing a potted plant in the centre of the boardroom table; the broad leaves filled the room; the magenta buds were just opening – their hearts were broken. Williams wanted to speak about his son – he said he had just buried him; Phillip was the one on whom the stones had fallen; his head had been crushed, his mouth filled. Exhaustion held Williams's lips together; his body slumped in the swivel chair; he remembered the years abandoned, without air, under the ground. Jacqueline's mouth drooped in silence. "They put him away," she said. "I am the one left above ground." Williams addressed Michael: "We committed a crime." "A crime? Even if it were…" Michael's lips were evasive as a game; he put his hand up to conceal a yawn: "You consider it a crime? And if it were?" Williams was a tall man; the expressionless face was the same; the beauty of those fat hands, the stale face red with eating, little eyes able to measure strangers – he could not keep his hands still; the face with fever hunted for shade. At eight thirty, half an hour later, Williams should have been prepared; the first weeks were for waking and prayers; he was covered with turf – with two stones a length apart; they will be praying again, now, one at each end; the land was quiet; little prayer herself, Williams saw Jacqueline's eyes on him; it seemed to him as if she looked down on him – the expression set in hostility. She asked if she was needed further; she understood their moods. Williams said he did not mind if she stayed, in a voice worn out with politeness. "What do you mean to do?" Michael asked his father. "Nothing." Jacqueline transcribed her shorthand notes; her mouth cut a line in three. Williams sat beside her on the couch. Michael said he was wanted in his office and must go at once.

Williams tried to talk to the girl; it was hopeless – he had forgotten her name. He handed her a note; she said he could not ask that of her; she would read the note – she accepted it – but she would not reply. Williams did not care whether his few lines offered her everything now, or nothing, year after year, for he had money, and when his pockets were pouring with money she would follow the scent of it home.

Jacqueline stood in the passageway, where Williams could see her; he waited, in repetition of his first mistake. He talked about love and honour while the messengers and other authorities pushed by. He spoke to her as to a familiar; she sighed; she went on exactly as before, busy with envelopes, her expression pleasant enough.

Williams was unwilling to meet his son – he had said what he had to say; he was businesslike; he did not refer to the matter again. When Williams's telephone rang, a recording replied: "He is not here now. I cannot say when he will be back." Williams sat on the floor; he was in unknown territory; he talked to himself: "I ask you – seriously…"

"That's bad," Michael said in the night air, and waited below the windows. Williams's position was weakening – his opponents were closing in; they threatened him. The glow of sunset was getting no nearer; a moment later the red turned black, then stopped. Two men turned up; Michael went towards them; they had come to see the old man shouting. The hair on Michael's head was angry, then he forgot about it. He thought as hard as he could: all that would come to mind was his brother and a dog sniffing his tie.

Respect for Michael increased – the men began to associate him with authority. Though Williams remained the father and the most famous, the founder of the firm, Michael raged more frequently, and in their homes his voice was heard. When banknotes rustled or furniture crashed, the son's voice continued to exhort and instruct, while the father stayed in the gloomy room. Michael relieved the image of the stern and barren man by promoting a rumour that he was planning to get married; his charm emerged clearly when he was seen practising dipping his finger into a ring – nothing could have been more natural. Michael even began to express concern at the half a million social casualties – the chronic sick, long unemployed, the widows, the separated wives. "We must rehabilitate the homeless, visit them in their homes." Williams attended meetings less frequently, as his troubles gathered and prepared for him. His portrait remained on the wall, and at times – hard times – men glanced at the face, the heavy head and shoulders on the wall. But Michael wielded power; old loyalties shifted to keep pace with latest developments. Michael signed letters and documents in his father's name "to ensure continuity of policy"; the younger man impersonated the older for as long as he was allowed; then the business and the family split. Each required the other to give way – one could not avoid humiliation. Each was obeyed in the absence of the other; all remembered the good old times when nobody doubted who was boss or gave a damn about respect or what to say on formal occasions, and no one walked with care. "Nowadays we watch our step; we prefer not to become involved."

Chapter 6

THE MIRRORED STEEL of the new building shone in the sun, noticeable from thirty miles away. Williams shut his eyes against the glare; it was a question of technique. According to plan, the factory was being transformed. Thermoplastic strips coalesced into the new symbol: an arrow wavering close to the head, the head protected by a helmet. The gaily striped workers revolved in cylinders; the appalling millions struggled for money. Accountants checked each operation; there was nil extravagance; no one walked in or out without cunning machines counting the cost. The new towers were cleaned and stripped, display windows wiped with a rag, glass doors opened without fuss; information was accurate and up to date; electronic minds worked ideally in the future. Bulldozers turned large stones over and sucked pebbles into themselves; the operators turned and talked in their sleep. Hundreds were killed, dressed, displayed: yellowish fat and lilac hair, crosses placed on the breast. The management celebrated their memory, proclaimed a holiday. The operation was organized to maintain profit margins; goods were sold for weeks at higher prices.

Williams escaped from the din. He drove to the river. The long machine flew soundlessly over the flowing lights.

In the centre of the arcade strong lights blazed, the rest dark. A rectangle enclosed a circle; chairs were placed in a ring. The bingo cries resounded through the hall; Williams looked bored – the look of a man who knows his name will not be called. The flying lights and clinking noise were entertainment for the people. He shot a steel ball, spent hours playing games, with fifty others sat in a semicircle; a head nodded, an arm froze. The band played 'The Blue Danube'. He joylessly clicked billiards, the game of boredom. He sat for an hour with a cup of coffee; he tried to get up; he put his hand out for a moment; his neighbours could not see his suffering. Promptly at two, Williams met Jacqueline, sitting there, as arranged. She stuffed a chocolate cake into her mouth as if she was pushing in a handkerchief; she wiped her fingers; she was brought a bowl of water to clean her fingers; she dropped silver paper on the floor, rubbed the crumbs from her fingers. Williams put on his glasses to read the bill. Her nail rested on her cheek; Jacqueline scratched her neck under her scarf; she made washing movements with her hands; prayed with them, clasped them together. Williams thought, "What that girl does with her hands is a complete ballet." The position of her fingers, the forefinger tapping. Williams leant forwards and said something. "Hmmmm." She could not hear what he said. He studied the bill. "I'll settle it." "Thank you." They got up together, faced each other; she turned and went back into the crowded arcade, and he followed.

He bought violets for her lapel. She knew how to thank him; his generosity entitled him to thanks, but she did not have to smile; she was no film star; she knew he had come for a reason. Williams asked her what religion meant. God was God, he said. He had spoken to Jesus Christ once, in the street; He had said He was born in Aberdeen. Jacqueline said she gave money to her mother; they lived as best they could. "You don't need much money to live. I wasn't born yesterday; I've done all the things there are to do – I mean, I've had all the nightlife – not recently, but before. I've done the lot. Now it doesn't interest me." She was attractive, dark-haired, compact, quiet, dressed in a black wool dress with red trimmings. Her father was nearly seventy-six; he was what was termed an "old man". He used to have a shop at the corner of Union Street – it had been three storeys high. She used words used in the street – hard or soft – she was not a woman, but a thing sold in the street.

The arcade was crowded with meaningless machines. Jacqueline said if she had her way she would break up and destroy all machines. Williams said, "If money is needed, we'll give a million." "A billion is better than a million." She was not interested; her mouth full of biscuits, she leant against him while he rambled on about his past. "My fingers were burnt – I lost money – three thousand at the races – I lost a packet; I quarrelled with them all." He lit a cigar; the smoke spread up to the canvas ceiling. "Wait, I'll show you a trick." He held her hand tightly. "I'll bet you a fiver." He spun a penny, threw another into the air. "See – it slips from the top; the finger in the centre of the change." He spoke of money with affection. "I swallow money. I play the fool, but I work the better for it." His face was lined with money; his business talent was remarkable. "The street was my home," Jacqueline said. "I stayed with my father till he failed. Then five pounds a night. I've tried to get out of that line. It's not easy to quit the business. I have travelled – I've been all over; I kept my family for years. I feel at home in the street; I've danced and sung in the street." "You're a funny girl." "My dress was dotted red and black. I greased my skin and dabbed on my war paint; there was good money around." Her short coat showed off the shape of her legs. Williams put a penny in a slot; a wire horse lit up, its eyes inspired with slow poison; the horse danced with two penguins on a chromium highway. At the moment the horse was reduced to ashes; fireworks went off. He did not know whether the coincidence was intentional, but the effect was "quite delightful"; stars shot up, spun about, shrieked and died away above their heads. "Green is the colour for stars; the manufacture is dangerous; chlorate provides the colour, sulphur the risk." The horse was an elaborate structure of wires which passed and crossed – life was the result – a small green blob, a load of damned rubbish masquerading as a miracle.

He took her back to the chauffeured car, determined to go anywhere at all; the glass wheels burst in the form of grey flowers. "You don't have any fun, that's your trouble," Jacqueline said, as the old man climbed slowly from the car – the ground was farther than it looked. Williams felt the nervous build-up for the prize – all the paraphernalia, her shrouded look, distant shouts, phrases repeated for effect. His mauve-lensed spectacles looked puzzled as the car was driven off, turned around, swept away and headed north-west, leaving him alone with the great assurance of her heavy hair, his shaky legs in the endless land, to kick a hole in the night. He could not show her moonlight: there was no moon. He showed her a tray of rings like bits of machinery, coordinated rings worn on the finger. She said, "It makes me nervous to think of rings. Hell to be seen with a ring." At five o'clock he pushed her to the ground and managed to kiss her. His attention was diverted by the calm with which she looked back at him, got up and rubbed her bruised arm. She stepped over him; she said she was hungry – she asked for fried fish and tea. "This is not a hotel." Then he put the questions; she gave the answers; she got bored; he began to enjoy himself. Her skirt had embroidered seams; one cheekbone was scratched; her hat lay on the ground – she held it for a moment, then walked away from the useless decoration.

When Jacqueline returned, her eyes trembled with pity; she leant forwards, displaying her bosom in her blouse. She offered her cheek; she pleaded with him to make love to her. He apologized for what had occurred. "Unable to comply with my bargains, bang, bang, bang." She said, "It's not your fault – you're worried." "There's a sort of ache in my back." "Why didn't you say? I can't guess these things." "I didn't tell you, but that's what is making me irritable." "I'll get you a cushion." "I don't need a cushion." She let him lie with his head in her lap. She located the pain and rubbed the small of his back.

Williams's earlier search for her had been successful; now she was disappearing, now she talked about her father. "Sad, white-haired and living at Teignmouth, he looks normal enough; at least he can walk quite well – it is slow, it is costly." Now a smaller bungalow, a small lawn; you can get a girl to do the cooking. Williams remembered her naked skin, her legs; the breasts pointed; her skin had a shine, a smoothness when wet. Her eyes were not simple; Jacqueline had reason to suspect his motives, evidence from her husband. Williams had not known Jacqueline in the remote past; she did not speak of Phillip and say "I miss him" – the memory of her marriage must have died. Her name meant she was his child; her first name came from her grandmother. Her generation and his were different – she was less sophisticated – the differences created barriers. The problem had been complicated by placing her next to Michael and allowing the two to touch. Now Michael maintained that he owned her; his claim was inadmissible. Williams and Jacqueline had contrived what they called their "connecting link", but it had become modified by time. When Jacqueline said she now wished to go back to Michael's house, Williams knew that she was closed to any other man by his son's hold on her; the old man knew that the younger occupied first place.

Chapter 7

WILLIAMS CHANGED his mind about visiting his son – he drove alone towards Michael's house; he had to turn right; his shirt was sweating under the armpits; it was too early – he would call in for drinks at ten; perhaps he would walk – walking was better for the health – but it would be foolish not to drive. The man from the lower ranks was staying put; the chief was coming to him; it was shameful.

The father arrived, ruffled, blustering, reluctant. He walked into the room, which was warm; there were two chairs, curtains, a carpet. Jacqueline was sitting on the floor near the fire, staring at the flames; her hair was hot; she wore a ring; Michael was beside her. It was the turn of the elderly man to be helped and held in a chair. Williams said to his son, "Like other relatives of the same species, we cannot be kept separate; you understand?" "I'm afraid I don't follow." "Can't you see it?" Their friendship was buried in irrelevant formality. Williams's fierce face, set and bleak, betrayed the division. He ought not to feel ill at ease in his son's house; this was not his son and never would be – the young man's eyes were his own; he must learn to understand; no one could be trusted. Michael turned towards the array of glasses and busied himself. Williams attempted to control the dual picture of the two sons, the lively and the vegetable death, the fighting boys. He took off his coat and went nearer to the fire. Williams said, "I will have a glass." His cold tone regarded the other man. "Shall I help myself?"

The whisky spread into the old man's neck and percolated down; warmth gradually returned. Williams needed to talk; the heavy shoes rested on the floor; the best thing he could do was keep talking without moving. He talked like a sickness; the cough came back to the bitter throat; he forgot there were things he should not have said. "Well, I'm glad I came" – looking round their room he had been in many times before, though without the light-backed woman, erect, seated at his table among the faces he had known. The young couple were discussing the different ways of making a good Martini, and Williams sat down again and listened to the benevolent game; he said he had once been a bartender, and had devised a means of increasing the profit on each drink – he would give them a demonstration of how to make a real gin sling. Michael produced a pack of cards, laid them face down and said they represented the letters of a name. He was beginning a line of seven letters on the table and saying they went like this when Williams got up and sat beside him, his black shoes next to the brown. "I can't sit on that chair," Williams said. Jacqueline's light lipstick made her lips look bare in the brightness which bisected the silver lining the mantelpiece, her bare brown legs half smiling in white linen shorts. Williams touched her knees and said, "They constitute temptation to the aged – a resting place for the fallen." They felt their intestines contract; the conversation halted. Williams bit the inside of his thumb; he made peace with laughter.

Williams mumbled out the cards with a bottle of whisky. "I'm a professional," he said; in the same tone he went on repeating the names of the cards with fury; they shot from the pack. "Let's get it over quickly." Michael felt a touch of shame. "Sorry – I'm dreaming." Williams held the cards with the broad, tough hands of an engineer; he sat low over the edge of the table, while they waited for a sign that he would get up and go. But he said he would show them a trick or two worth knowing. "Mark one side of the card with a dot or a pip. A chalk mark will serve." He said he would read Jacqueline's palm; his eyes scoured the hand for the lines of her past. "I haven't the secret. So there we are." Williams caught her glance at Michael and avoided the implied invitation for him to go. "I can read the face but not the palm," he said; "well, I'll try, but you must cooperate. I want to see your mouths cancelling the words I pronounce: father or brother or husband might do it." Williams longed for some reaction or other to bring the war into the open in the family – individuals in the heat of conflict, like the leaves on a tree variously tinted by the hot edge of summer.

From indecision Williams stayed. The role of the eldest living child was played as Michael stared down at his drink, into his own palm. "A man is no more than a bag of bones," Michael spoke without motive. "As a father perhaps you can cure this yearning for power, and the consequent pain in the kidneys?" Picking the hearts on the cards between his finger and thumb, tracing the squares on the table as if the missing cards were still set out, Michael said solemnly, "There are possibilities and probabilities as to the disappearance of the table and the disintegration of the family, and the table hath disappeared."

Williams looked through the misted windows at the lights of the town spread out in the night; he shared the stump of a cigar with his son, and after two or three false starts talked sensibly about the rebuilding of the factory. Then his words slowed; he played with two coloured pencils, making marks on their scorecards – either red or blue. "My temperament – no, my life doesn't matter, but I thought I could squeeze a living," Williams said. "In business you ease out slowly, waiting for your sons to take over. I must go away and think; thirty years' work have been enough."

An old man with his hat in his hand, the hands in black-string driving gloves, Williams was in the position of kneeling in his son's room, in his son's house – the charming house looking onto the river. The contest would last for years – for longer than that.

The billowing cloud of memory Michael held for her as he held her hand; her sad eyes, the young skull on her lap, the floating skirt of sand, the arm growing from the sky, the pyjama jacket, bow tie at the neck, as Michael looked forwards and she looked back.

"Grant me one gift." Williams had begun his fall; he stumbled on the skull; he would try again when she felt hungry. The peacocks screamed in his dream: "I knew you would come." The wreckage of the garden, the curtains of the house. He would end – moving on a few steps.

"Not long ago," Williams said, "I went to Michael's room when he was asleep. I leant over him and took a key from his pocket. I opened his desk and found hundreds of love letters. I could hardly believe it – what did they mean to him? After reading for hours by torchlight I found what I was looking for – I knew it was time to change my plans." They stared at him, saying nothing. "Do you wonder, Michael, why Jacqueline here sobbed on my shoulder after the funeral? She was practically unconscious after the long nightmare; she fell on the floor; I put my arms around her and offered her a cigarette; 'I don't want to worry you, Father,' she said, with a look of true contentment. I could see the fear slip from her as if I were turning the pages of a book and the grey print brightened with colour. The life came back into her body; she looked as if she had attended not a funeral, but a feast."

The angled light cut her shoulder and connected her with the young man's hand, demonstrated the isolation of the pair before the impending storm. The young couple held hands; they were celebrating; they went together – they announced their intention to marry. Each, ready for duty, supported the other, the man in front and prepared to deal quickly with trouble, while she walked in the garden, following the wall close to the house, for her dress to be seen in a crescent; the pace was slow and the white flowers twined in her romantic hair, and she was so happy and cared almost nothing for the crowd's chatter or the father's disapproval.

"Can we go out tomorrow?" Jacqueline asked, and Michael thought, "Take her out, now – immediately; manage it, be with her; whatever she wants to; make up to her with gratitude and kisses." "I've got a surprise for you." She looked up eagerly. "It's beautiful, this moment, to uncover happiness. We'll have a good time today," she said. "You can stay till morning." He wagged his finger at the laughing face, the swinging lines of her hair.

Williams turned into the wind, with hat and coat; it made him more set on getting away this week – a tremendous joy it used to be – no, he was playing with pictures. Alone this evening, perhaps yes, but of course she would want his congratulations. His age and eyes could not possess or be possessive; as he went out of the gate, he had lost her looking at him. "I'd like you to approve," she had said. "Well, well, we shall see."

In his office Williams sat in his chair; his unhappiness alarmed him. He was impatient; his hands merged in a spire – cuffs shabby, spotted with acid; he examined his hands without realizing whose they were, thinking he should be kind to them, as he received a message that could not be forwarded in a voice that would not come back. His sight grew better – he could see the clock on the wall. He said to Jacqueline, "You'll marry him?" She joked: "Who can have told you?" Then, after she had looked at him for a moment, he said, "I'll help you both."

Williams could manage the stairs without her help, but the boots were too large, or the laces broken. He needed to ask certain questions. The descending shiny stairs at the same pace turned left through a door – there was not a room, only a region smelling of acid. The floor regarded him; Jacqueline left him with the door painted green, the hot wood smoking. Williams could have opened the door and gone outside; the door remained open with hinges on red and green, and the ends of iron smiled as at a party; he could see the wide-open smile in which teeth glistened after rain; the slack muscles of his mouth were the texture of melting ice; he felt the warm fluid running over his cheeks. When Jacqueline came back through the door, she could not recognize his eyes, which had changed colour and changed shape. She brought him a glass of boiled water; he drank to move the muscles of his mouth; he could speak more easily; the thick lips pushed between her hands. "This is the last outpost of civilization. I'll hold you here with my teeth." He split matches lengthwise, swearing slowly. She said he was expected to give away the bride; she asked him his full name and wrote it down; she told him where the ceremony was to be held, and when, and gave him the ring to hold.

Williams watched the needle waver uncertainly; Jacqueline was trying to steady the details, her mirror constantly with her; the scent of powder: he felt her nerves contract, death between them, probing the sullen fire. He said it was stupid and pointless – he was more than sixty years old; she was less than half his age; he talked about the distance kicking the edge of the day, the edge of change. She said, "I haven't got all day." He replied, "I'm staying here till…" Jacqueline detested his hands fidgeting in his pockets. Williams said, "I'd like some hot milk." She heard him talking to his imaginary companion – the sound that came from his chest: "I cannot for the life of me remember – it's gone, the trouble is. Look at this: an axe head found in a field, before history; all these things remind you of the olden days." "I'd like to have seen that. Are you sure it is stone, not bone?" "I've thought that before. I like that thing, the way it catches the light; I've been wanting you to see it for so long," Williams said. "You know, you don't need to wear that suit all day," she said. "I don't like it – you look funny in it." He had been trying to describe the axe head; he stopped talking about it. "I feel like some fresh air – it's very bad to be cooped up; I've got too many clothes on; I'm used to being out in all weathers. If I go to sleep again I'm bound not to sleep at night," he said. "You would sleep better in the evening; you pack too much sleeping in during the day." "I need to keep occupied. I'm getting too much sleep during the day. I've got to learn to sit in that chair without dreaming. You should not have left me for an hour with the fire on. You look nice in that dress – refreshing to the eye. You help me up now." "Heavy, aren't you." "Quite heavy." "What are you up to now? What's going on?" Williams lay a long time in the same position on the couch – one leg extended towards the wall, the head craned back, staring at the ceiling. Her pleasure came from seeing him asleep with his lips bent in a curve of loneliness; it was the only time she was not afraid of him. She wanted to put her arm round him, but did not wish to wake him; she raised his head and he did not wake, and she was able to crouch there, watching him. Jacqueline moved her head so that her hair touched his face, and he woke. He bent over and enclosed the part below – simple, soft part, the inside of a fish; later and lower, the cave in the wall, discovery. "If he asks me to marry him, I shall." She lay on her side while he pierced the wall that separated them; there was a division of labour – they were both important and remarkable; they formed a pair. In his mouth lay her ear; he shifted and she could see the nostril – a pit above the mouth. Williams felt a pain at the side of his head; Jacqueline a sense of pity, depression; it was dark; she could feel his face; the parts of her body seemed separate. Jacqueline thought she slept. Williams heard her talking about him like a ship sinking. "I'm staying with you." She got up and went to the lavatory and washed herself. When she came back he was sitting in his chair, his feet on the rungs, in the middle of the room on his own. "What are you doing here? You must have something better to do?" he said. She looked away, while he went through the mechanical motions of work with all the excitement of his body, one shoulder forwards; he spoke of a house and wife and his sons, and from the tension in the fat face he might have been back at work, except for the eyes, which were not fully open. His mind was held by some inward strain from the past, but he liked his belly full; this amused her – he kept on asking for more food, and however much she gave him, his plate was returned empty. The office was barely lit, for Williams's commanding presence demanded drawn curtains; the gloom began to affect her nerves. He insisted on the windows remaining closed. In the summer he had seen a bluebottle beating against the glass, and had fallen badly in his efforts to let it out. He said, "If you had valued my son Phillip's memory, you would not have married again." She was too secretive to answer; she merely nodded.

The stroke of seven died. Williams saw the watch fixed to her wrist; she had been looking out at the yellow fog slipping; her face was so nearly fine; the narrow lights appeared to plan the colours of the pavement, the hurried railings, the slam of temper at the door; her feet sensed a reluctant animal, a man's grip in every direction. Michael said, "I'm glad I was in time." Jacqueline felt her face tighten, the scrape of her chair. "I want to tell you…" her voice died; the sound of the fog beyond the walls. "I must tell you. I do not wish to come here again."

When Michael said he would go home alone, Jacqueline asked to go with him. She dabbed her face with powder; she was still a woman. "It's nice to get out of this place." Her lips apart, a pair of dirty yellow gloves squeezed together between houses and covered with rubbish.

From the window, Williams watched them down the street; he gave them time. In the open air he remembered her toneless voice in the closed room. The works of a pavement artist were lined up against a wall; now it was quite possible he didn't paint them himself – ye glens and lochs with the most ghastly lurid lights. Williams wondered: did anyone buy them? He supposed so – simple souls. It was winter: cold air covered the sides of cars and low buildings, street lights lit the wide road, the dry pavement with its coating of dust a few millimetres high; the quiet buildings lined the road, the objects, telephone kiosk, pillar box, were touched by the cold. At one point the monotony was broken. In the centre of the road a heap of stones were piled one on another; a few tufts of grass grew among the stones. In the square brick house, on a bed, the girl slept in her clothes.

Chapter 8

THE CATHEDRAL HAD the walk of a woman in
love. Their alcoholic wedding flowed jubilant and
huge down the turbulent aisle. The scarlet carpet led
Michael and Jacqueline to the altar of gold; the shining
cross rose and wavered and fell; the desperate choir rose
painfully, their treble soft and soundless, the vaulted
ceiling thin with song. The broad columns ruled the
building; the nave had windows, walls and chairs. Even
a telephone. The storm outside swept the slates loose
from the ancient roof; the guests in the graveyard shouted
"Goodbye!" Williams in a silk hat, a beard on his chin:
they left him alone. His greatcoat was covered in fur;
the sad beard shielded his eyes; there was no room for
him; he was covered in fur, like a kitten; his beard covered a mole – the mole was a novelty at the corner of
his mouth; he stood in the corner and they bid him
goodbye. They put on lights; the building was lit on
three sides and surrounded by fairy lights; the wind
blew; the roof shook; the priest intoned and the choir
sang; the building trembled and the stained glass shone
onto the stone floors, and the unseen waves of the sun
made the ancient slates vibrate as the thoughtful faces
broke against the floor.

The verger put up the metal shutters to stop the panes from falling out; they had closed the windows in the morning to keep the cool air in. The nervous groom hiccupped in the morning; for five minutes Michael jerked at speed; Jacqueline was miserable and slapped his back; the contest between them continued – he jerked, she slapped – till the force of the woman won. The famous bride with the pretty ears: her breasts bulged under her wedding gown; a drop of saliva dripped from her mouth; her chin in her palm, eyes on the cross.

The bride and groom ate the bread and wine; the warm wine made them belch; the chalice kept sliding off the cloth; the bread was made to be eaten. The bride hung over the altar rail; she belched; the choir waited and were quiet – they were not allowed to sing. In the chancel the fat little boys sat on pillows stuffed with hair; they sat with straight backs, playing with marbles at their feet, furtively rolling the marbles about. The congregation waited in rows of pews divided by pillars from the main nave, while the bride cried before the cross. As best man, Williams slipped in to flourish the ring; his technique was bold; the slim lines of his body swung as he faultlessly executed the necessary bow. He had known better days – much wealth, little art, more's the pity. His fingers flicked at the ring; he added "the ghost of a smile" – just right. The clergy wore hats and badges, waited with folded arms. The groom flopped on his knees; the bride stopped slapping his back; the best man gave the groom, gave the bride the ring; Williams rehearsed his bow; the window panes, smashed by the wind, on the floor; the congregation was overjoyed with its toys.

Jacqueline opened the book while the silk light touched her fingers with a slight sound. Her hand and purpose was to convince Michael that the man who had died was nothing to her, because when death came it stayed. Kneeling side by side, their faces in the shadow cast by the cross, they could not move from their place. Michael closed his mind. Jacqueline attempted to edge away from the smell of sour meat pies. Williams stared at the strip of silk that edged the bodice of her wedding dress, shifted his religious glance to her face. Her hands on her lap, she waited; it was a waste of time; the priestly voice was lost in space; mildew clung to the ancient ceiling; the stone gave no warmth. Michael bent over his bride's face and wiped the eyes with his handkerchief. The thought hung in the face; she heard his voice answer against the steady hum compounded of vague, curious noises; two voices heard: one deep, one high. Jacqueline watched Michael speak to the priest – question and answer went outside and merged with a girl passing. The bride's body was trembling; her eyes fluttered like pet mice; she loosened her silvery dress. "It's terribly bright – too bright for the occasion." "It suits you – it's lovely – you're so dark." Williams smiled encouragingly; the bride answered the marriage lines; she hid her mouth with her hand; she had not been heard by a soul.

The congregation held on to their hats and picked up their wives from the floor; they peered at the cross with hope; the incense left a pillar of smoke in the vacant church in the world. The steel seagulls turned; the steeple pushed into the sky; a small green tree emerged in a cloud on the right; the cathedral stopped in its tracks, stealthy, incomprehensible, huge.

The wooden pews contained the wooden men: each was examined by all; each tapped on the chest – resounded like a bell, a coin – hollow, perfect, sold. The bride stuck out her ordinary tongue, wet her lips, pink and gleaming, worrying the anxious priest. Because of his inexperience, he glanced at the silly girl, her breasts swinging, and the incense swung back and forth till he quieted down a little. Not so noticeable, she knelt before the altar, examining her nails. Her attempt to make him look had failed. Sex between a priest and lady: grace before the feast. The choir sang their songs, played their ancient game; from time to time they stopped; a dog barked, a coin clinked, one rubbed his foot, or something hindered them. Whenever they stopped, she smiled.

As Michael knelt by the flat-topped block for offerings to the deity, the long music resounded, and the older man had been beaten by the younger. Williams knelt as the white arms were raised; the father murmured as he fell; he behaved as if the issue of the fight had not been determined; he grumbled constantly through the service; they thought it was prayer. Williams swung his arms, clasped his hands together, knelt on the cushion, while the priest continued his beautiful monotone according to the order of the service and the rules for making his living. The praying man shoved his fingers into his mouth, scratched the wood with his nails; this was not permitted; the congregation took an interest in it; Williams was a sinner in hell. He tried to break his nail by jamming it in the spokes of the chair in front; no harm was done – the chair was moved away. There were no chairs left near him; they laid clean sand on the floor. The old man sat on the sand and blew his fingers; he raised his hat in greeting;

he waved with incredible persistence; he lay on his back as long as possible; he did not want to disgrace his name; he crawled round in a circle, lay still on the stone floor. Michael put down his little book and hurried to his father with a speed one would not have expected from a man in formal dress; he spotted the miserable sinner and came down in a flash; he grabbed the older man and forced him off the ground; after ten minutes' hidden struggle he succeeded. Michael pulled a small crucifix from his pocket and presented it to the mournful man as he led him to the barrier, so that the father was forgotten and put in a room beneath the stairs where he could not be seen. Michael's brilliant gesture with the cross made the congregation forget the tear-smeared face and the bruised lips and eyes.

The bride stood lovingly over the cross. Round her neck hung a cross. She looked young and cheap. She knelt on the stone floor, which was covered with patterned carpet. The carpet over the mosaic floor weighed half a ton. Jacqueline prayed for the first time in her life: it was significant, a great event.

After the service the transparent light hung over her. A short distance away the waiting priests played chess; one read the day's papers; the other bent down, placed a captured knight beside a bible on the floor. An elbow knocked a bowl of wine, which spilt on the stone. Above, the stained glass glowed with sun: a red light shone on the floor; the set faces turned towards the eventful spot. Jacqueline thought she should walk to the altar to study, observe, take note. She ran there at speed; she stepped in the wine on the floor. Blue eyes, pretty ears, pink lips: the priests regarded her suspiciously; their joyless eyes gazed not at her, but at Him. "By suffering, how else communicate faith?" the bishop intoned. He studied the list of the rich – the twelve richest; God was a wealthy man; he sang on the radio. The portly bishop in the grey suit: his head was grey, his hands small and smooth; he held an object made of plastic: the pornographic bosom of a star. He said nothing had changed. He wished the couple every happiness. He seemed anxious to get away; the pews were empty; it was the end of his day. But the bride and groom would see him again; he decided to use those last minutes; he picked a last remark. "I am not too well. It was the war." Their answers were not much help – he was trying to show that Christ was up to date: He read the papers, but he could not decide which side He was on. On contraception he was cagey; he stood up and said otherwise; the panel of experts was now examining the problem. "My position on the bomb, inclined against the pill" – waiting for the holy father in charming fashion, carried a cine-camera slung beneath his lace. Christ had allowed a man to walk; the plank had reached the door; the noisy boards had masked the door; along the passage in the dark, the day trip in the dark, something moved across the floor; the movements stopped when Christ said stop. The priest with kindly eyes, Michael's elbow in his hand, his hand on Jacqueline straying, he steered them to the door; he warned that the future might be hard. The couple posed for the customary photograph: the two looked straight at the camera, and Williams in the photo had his hands up.

Chapter 9

S HAPED BY THE ROSY affirmation natural to people
who own new cars, the happy couple were shown to
the crowd, but the trick did not work. The steel sun covered herself with snow; the workers barely raised their
heads; it was a matter of fatigue. This slackness lasted an
hour – it divided the men from their work; it reduced their
value. To Michael this was a sign that it was a time for
culture and for art. A holiday would release the men; they
would dance round a tree. When the novelty wore off, the
taxes could be increased; the law would remain in force;
the people would be sheltered from the blast of peace.

Not a twitch on the face of the bored constable, whose
deadpan expression turned towards the crowd that was
egging him on. Beneath the intractable gaze, a woman
patted her headscarf with white gloves, a hard-faced man
with regimental tie said he did not intend to be home
till two. There were well-wishers too. At five o'clock the
joyful couple were asked to step outside. To fusillades of
flashbulbs and shouts of "God bless you, sir" and "We're
with you, Mr Williams", like stars ducking, Michael and
Jacqueline turned their backs as the crowds swarmed, and
their car revved up and swirled off towards the square.
In the public gardens at nine in the morning, before the

pubs opened, the crowds arrived to drink the nourishing beer. The men took off their jackets; they had come from their different jobs, and at seven forty-five they disturbed the district with the purposeful rattle of railings. There was fun in their faces; a thirsty queue formed round the garden; the gardeners looked in envy; the head gardener closed the gates, and soon the plush and straining ropes held in the crowd's common determination; they were not all young; the coaches kept rolling up to discharge their loads over the hedges; they were going to have a wonderful time; the pace of the early hours would make climbing the stairs hell by evening; still more honest workers arrived – to hell with the licensing laws! – and so to pleasure. There was another reason for the general gaiety; they seemed almost grim as with determined step; hell-bent on this hilarious morning, with added mateyness, they thrilled with the sense of sin. There were few lone children at play or pleasure; naturally there was one huge insistent party as the trains put down their passengers and the coaches collected the crates of beer. Williams and Michael drank large whiskies with beer as a cleansing chaser; Michael brought his bride and sat her in the corner of the garden. On every chair was a can of beer, and as the morning went on the garden became barricaded with crate after crate; barrels were opened and emptied and used as seats. At the centre of the alcoholic typhoon, the tempo warmed as they piled themselves on tables and the stomachs, heavy with beer, turned towards the afternoon sun. Out came swarms of bees, and the lovers liked it hot, and were found in corners with their passionate sandwiches wrapped in greaseproof paper. Someone said "Now!" and off came their skirts with the sun; the embarrassed gleam of white skin was hidden by hills of bottles as the music took possession of them all with the whole range of Spanish vibrations and clever guitar strings. Williams's jacket was off, and his tartan braces down; before the afternoon was over the garden gates were open to the town; everybody brought tomato sandwiches, and a hundred pairs of welcoming arms embraced and carried on drinking. By nine thirty the queues wound round the garden before every barrel of beer; whole families came, with great weights of potato crisps, and Everyman had a pickled onion belching out his past. Hairy-chested Williams proudly showed his chest. Those not in the family on the hot and Sunday morning, with a potent bottle in each hand, joined the club and brought along the bottles and shook hands with friends. Jacqueline joined some jolly girls bobbing up and down, and there were people who came to the party who had not previously had the pleasure, jerking and bending with greetings and singing, standing hour after hour. The family included outsiders and other congenial companions. Jacqueline was up again in a white frill of cotton, and she knew a trick worth two of that in the widening circle; she was dressed to kill, and for this came the crackle of the loudspeaker: "Attention, please!" And she was awarded the prize, and she said she was pleased, and they were twelve marvellous hours.

At Michael's home the fashionable party proceeded. Jacqueline's two pink shoes danced with Michael's two black shoes; hers followed his, side by side, like a child clinging to its parents. When he mistimed the beat and led her impatiently to the exit, he received her opaque eye; her short questing nose pointed at his as they took turns showing each other the steps; she swept him back in a tumble of words and gestures, explaining the steps and the rhythm. Clumsily handsome, Michael stretched that elegant neck like a chick breaking through its shell. He put his hand in hers: "I'll soon get the hang of this." Jacqueline pretended to be fluffy, helpless, and her inert little body darted away as though with his mistakes he had ruined the intimate party. Williams flung his cocktail exultantly into the air, in order to know the glass at the moment of crisis, regarded the girl – her slim arms almost as light as her stockings; he did not shrink in the anonymity of the music when a circle of trumpet expanded across the room. Williams and Jacqueline were on their own, apart from the watching guests. Each glance remained a character, the moth-eaten appearance of a kiss. Then, her lips waves, she came to him and he to her. The extraordinary kiss was seen; the explosion was unquestionable. She tried to eject the tongue – it would become embarrassing. His tongue was short, then elongated; no explanation was offered. The tongue did not return; it was dispersed in space – grown and lost, like eight million tongues, wasted. This theory was offered: if they are wasted, their numbers must diminish; they must be preserved, remain in the family – members one of another. Once a tongue moves outside the family, it dies. She felt the tongue had a stony shell; the inner composition was not known. The presence of fluid could be explained: the deep mouth contained life, microscopic animals, one upon another. The probing of his tongue was hard; she wished it to become fluid – why is not known. When the skulls of men are found, there is only bone. Ideas were offered, guesses made. Some supposed the son allowed the father at different times. Others conjectured tension in limited space, war in the home, or agreed definitions of warmer and cooler areas. No physical explanation could be found for these hypotheses. Michael was rigid; his tense axis could not be shifted. If he had been elastic he could have been shifted, by means of a very slow process. The true cause was seen by few; the increase of love, the love set free, the action of family love was not considered. Ancient relationships both expanded and hindered; the myth created and obstructed; the contradiction would cause the fall.

Jacqueline was stopped by a man with a camera and a man with a notebook; they came to her for titbits; she was asked her story. "My father was a famous pianist; I was the daughter in his house." "Your father was a famous pianist; your background—" "Well, it must have been musical – I was five years old. Like nothing in the world. I was born. My father was. I had a governess who. She said, 'Well, don't you think you'll ever be as great as your father?' Well. But I went to the pictures, and liked them very much." "Was it a career for you?" "Oh, I enjoyed it, yes." "Will you make a success of your marriage?" "Oh, if this is a success, I will go on for ever doing the same thing." "Is this wickedness entirely assumed?" "Oh." "What is the essential quality of the excitement you wish to enjoy?" "Oh, I don't know. I am very happy because I do not have to. So full of enthusiasm, more or less. In the beginning I was too young." "Your friends, are they amusing in themselves?" "Not all." "Did anyone influence you greatly?" "No, no. One was dark and one was old. When he was smoking a cigarette he said, 'Kill it.' It was his idea of power." "Do you think this quality, this ability?—"

"He always loved to bring people together; the day I saw J.P. Macavoy, the writer. The most colourful personality in the world. It is necessary to be ruthless in any walk of life. Yes. I'm only interested in winning. That's the only way you're going to do it. I don't know whether anyone can say how far you can go, really." "Would it be fair to say you enjoy fighting?" "Oh yes, I love a fight. Get in. That's what I feel. At least you've got some satisfaction."

She did not think of Michael again in the midst of the hullabaloo of the curtains falling; the young body at the end of the party: the thighs were sweet as Williams moved the skirt away, close to his suit. Despite the fact that the time was wrong, she was very active and demanding. Meanwhile, with a face of ice, Michael waited by the door; he maintained his dignity while guests fought for their coats. Her hectic breasts trembled as Williams's fingers folded over them for six minutes, standing there in the tremendous commotion.

Chapter 10

THE WIFE'S LIFE CHANGED. Instead of an artist working alone, Jacqueline was continually asked what she was thinking. "Why do you stand around talking? The film starts in an hour." Or, in relation to friends or patrons, the design of the furniture in her home, her worship of God – or was it stone? Jacqueline was asked to hurry, and was invariably late. She discovered that her husband was a small man with fair hair. She became one of the trend-setting gossips. Whom she worshipped or why she worshipped him, everyone asked. Sometimes she said it was the way he put on his glasses, the way he moved. She was haunted by hangers-on in a search for originality; she soon found she could answer those fashionable questions; those that were taboo she discussed slowly and talked quietly, so that it was difficult to hear – and this, combined with the in-group fighting, made things meaningless to her. Jacqueline was still not clear what was being done. She asked, "If a thing is made in half an hour, why is it bought and sold as if it took a year?" She wished to know why one person had a replica of himself in continuous huge close-up installed in his lounge, as if it were man-magic, as if to touch the cardboard made one well. Why did he live with himself?

Why not a woman? If a product was supposed to sell for three hundred pounds, why could it not be sold for three hundred? After ten minutes' discussion of this point with a man who had made four fortunes, and an argument with a few people who could not answer her, it was this meta-physical girl arranging hairpins in her hair who decided in a voice flushed with failure that it all seemed to depend not so much on manufacture and other creative activities as on supporting a sound system which told her she was to be given success. Privately she acquired the legendary phrases, like "I have just strangled my pet Duchamp".

Jacqueline spent her time picking up objects from shops. She bought her dolls from a man who made figures of wax. Their heads were small, with coloured faces deco-rated with elastic threads of glue. She picked up a doll and put her thumb to its nose: "The thing is a stick and a piece of leather, and this is a ball of putty. Does it looks like a man? Where's its head and nose?" Michael said the heads were made in Hamburg; many were sad rubbish. She said she loved these ancient toys; she adored the feel of dolls in her arms – armless dolls with pretty faces, in lace jackets and velvet boots, the hats painted blue.

Jacqueline achieved the personality of a star, rather than the reputation she deserved – that of a person of common quality. Occasionally she startled her guests by singing, and once she sang a man to sleep for hours; this was such a success that she did it again and again. She was reported as saying that she preferred quite ordinary objects – eating a banana for instance; the papers took an interest in her performance; she became the mediator between the "strange" and the "hostile"; she was said, if you please, to be "imbued with wit and magic" – she called it "magicalicity". She kept bowls of sand and empty shells in her room, and a bleak humped photograph of Jackie in a tribal village dance. There were her bracelets, and the ceiling covered with purple stars; thirty reporters were waiting for her; she pulled off her dress and allowed herself to be loved by people who did not exist, as the young woman brushed her hair; this was fashion, not publicity – her uncreative mind fluttered her nipples and pouted her hair.

In the front garden of their home, Michael faced away from the front door, towards the iron gate set in the hedge. He carried a suitcase filled with Phillip's clothes. One hand held the case, the other empty. He put the case down and took a newspaper from his raincoat pocket. He kissed his wife and asked how he should dispose of the clothes. Jacqueline gave him aspirins – made him gargle, to hear the sound in his throat. They could not live with the boy who died. Michael took sleeping pills, talked about himself and the size of the world. He said she should have burned the clothes. "It's nothing – his hat or gloves are nothing to me," she said. "I never thought" – Michael went to the head of the stairs – "it is so long since there was a sound from below. Shall we talk about him?" "I think you ought to," Jacqueline said. "I'll be back soon; you stay – I'll be all right; we have so much time." Michael pulled another chair to the table. "You mean he?..." As she placed a jar of potted meat beside him, she would have a good hunt for some salad. Michael hurried his food. She took his plate before he was finished. "I can't tell you how nice the meal was," he said. "All right! If you don't like it. You've waited for something to happen. I can't keep you here. There's no sense. Does anyone care what happens in doctors' surgeries?" Michael went towards her, eyes puckered – the light was too bright; she ran forwards; he did what he could, at least; she said no, kept turning her head round. They were silent for an hour in memory of Phillip's long-playing records, a description of the smile he wore – that kind of thing; he kept the records in a case, not on the table; he entered the numbers in a book – careful, remember he had certain qualities – the game with the radio, long solitude, things of that sort; they had lived together. "I wrote him letters – you heard about them, I suppose?"

Fumbling for himself, Williams ate lunch alone. He could not remember where his overcoat was. Machinery roared; his spoon scratched the plate; the contrast stared at the clock, a perpetual light illuminated the whirling hands. Williams had his office separated from the others by a partition; in his room – the stubborn man – he tried not to sleep, to avoid growing old, lest he be caught off his guard. He kept Jacqueline's photograph on his desk, and pointed with a pencil when anyone called; they were made uncomfortable; his predicament could not be explained; no one thought aloud. Engrossed in his own health, Williams could spare little time for work.

Michael kept sane, ate cakes and told marvellous stories. The men respected him because he grew rich – thus he increased his fortune: he was tenth on the list of the rich. Michael's name was justly celebrated; his style advanced; his teeth had a vivacity of their own – hugely successful teeth – sales half a million.

Williams conceived crazy ideas: to train the workers by electricity. They were to be ordered to move and they would move, to stop and they would stop. They might play dead. Then, like small white animals, they would run away, squeeze into their tiny cells – impossible to feed them – no room for the scrap of food – they would complain persistently.

The old man became a memory, a name without distinction. He gained a reputation for being unhappy – he made his friends unhappy; apart from that he was unknown. Williams tried to keep his name alive, maintained the cult – his notepaper printed at the firm's expense, the concrete plate in the floor, the print of feet. He was the same man, with fur on the outside. He rolled along the road he could not see, across the dirt, to resurrect the old times, the poverty and absurdity. On his head was a cap; he began to shout he was old – age was nothing to youth – the bald head fell across the chair. He recalled when he had demonstrated the first lamp of the new type that burned around the world, the thread that would not break; he attached the lamp; he could not speak – he whistled; he spoke like a child and ended in laughter. He cursed work: the times had not been right; he had not had a chance. "I'll show you – you don't know a thing."

For a long time, Williams could not find his way among the constellation of unknown corridors; he seemed stationary, wandered around, played with matches; he felt his way as an automobile drives down a street of closed windows. He noticed there were no lights from the old factory; when he looked up, the lights on his side went out. Someone had operated the master switch. He remembered when nearby every lamp hung a chain; to turn off the light you held the end of the chain – a pull on the little chain and the light was pulled out. When the last workers had gone home, Williams began looking for the button that controlled the lights, and at that moment there was no button. In his old office Williams found the furniture and the old-fashioned lamps guarding it; a brown-looking, scarcely visible light trickily painted the old portable chair. He sat in his chair – a fat old woman whose time was limited, yet comfortable.

Williams feared that when he breathed so deeply that he sat bolt upright his chin would spring out of control. The machine had been tested and gone badly; the neck tendons showed the strain; his breath drawn in, he gripped the handle in his attack on the world. The maximum had been reached – exceeded. He talked to two men within five feet of him; someone provided a chair; his red hands gripped the white chair; the weather was bad – it was not fair. "I'll give her eighty-five; watch the dial." One of those grey-haired men with a serious face said success depended on numbers and power; the temperature was too low. "Switch on the radio and forget it – pack it in." Williams bent closer to the set; waltz time; his long black coat like an undertaker, he suggested they run the machine more slowly, to magnify each fault and make analysis possible. "It can be done" – furiously digging his toes in the rubble, rubbing the back of his neck, the sound grew; his heavy breath dug furrows in it, made a dent an inch deep, but the wheel had no intention of moving. "I was born to succeed – a successful man makes a track like a meteor," Williams said. It sounded easy, the opening and closing of the valves of the heart. As the machine shuddered, Williams looked as if he would shake to pieces. "What I would say to you, gentlemen… officially I would say to you men…" – the formalities continued, at slow speed, forty words an hour; he would go on – "…my opponents use consistent tactics – it is war – all weapons against me. I too use tactics. They anticipate feeble resistance, but we shall turn the tables. We have had ill luck from the start; our opponent has no scruples – a man who crosses the room to avoid a meeting. But I am determined – if it is said that murder would have a frightful effect – none the less, in the course of time…"

Rubbing the flask against his cheek, Williams coaxed a drop into his mouth – heaven; shut the door behind. He pulled his pockets inside out; the last drops hazed his being; swarms of flies darkened the corners of the windows; he threw the bottle among a clutter of others. "There's no money in it" – his eyes fixed. From outside the door: "That you?" Head slumped onto the desk, he hurried into sleep; his nose twitched with pleasure. He rubbed his nose – a clucking sound. "I'm sorry to wake you, dear" – Jacqueline's voice. He was glad of it. "I reported you ill; I had to think quickly. You might have warned me." Jacqueline's clean hands smelt of surgical spirit, soft lips folded over. "I've forgotten something," he said. "I'm here to help," she whispered.

Sunlight hit the corner of Williams's desk on time – reached over it inch by inch, spoke softly of brown butter, swung across Michael's voice on the phone: "I'm not concerned with details; perhaps you should be more careful – move a trifle closer to the community – what do you think?" Williams tried to frame the reply to his son, but the film of whisky stayed like rain; he studied his fingernails, heard a bus in the street below. "…Must not impede the spring production drive…" The faint sound of a pressed bell; reluctant answers touched upon his crimes; stolen money lay across his face.

"I would not go down yet – the panic is still on," Michael said, from his father's chair. Something like pain became the tight pulse in the centre of the room. Each sat in his place. Father and son "filled identical habitations" – the one confined in his place, the other held him there. "Children must be stopped from stoning dogs, and vermin washed from their hair," Williams said. "I do not accept instruction from one who knows less than myself," Michael replied.

His handkerchief stained red, Williams's voice tapped on the clean floor which his cold eyes suppressed; his fingers jerked into Jacqueline's face; she was not beautiful – she had let go, "desperate for love", from whatever motive. Williams promised her a car, on one condition: she must not tell Michael. Jacqueline wondered why she bargained with her lover over what she should say to her husband. She appeared excited at the prospect of a row; this angered Williams, yet money for the car was deliberately put into her pocket. She regretted the joy in her reply; she would not bother to tell Michael. "Do you mean that?" She would probably tell him some time – she could not conceal it. Williams said he would throw her out of his room – settle with her that night. He realized what day it was – Tuesday – what had happened that day – his promise of money, the six thousand pounds; his arms stretched and made an arc of importance; he said he understood her curiosity, her anxiety, her desire to make trouble. The slammed door cut out the light – the yellow wood edged with black.

Jacqueline remembered the tear in Williams's shirt. Thick tufts of hair stuck out of his nose as she sat on a stool mending his shirt. The young woman in the wide straw hat decorated with daisies; the white-lipped woman, beltless and shivering, the years abandoned in the place without air between the floor and the ground. Williams said, "First: my work is no good. I make a profit from men. The crime is recorded; our profits have risen ten per cent. I buy a man for less and sell him for more – that is a cheat, that is all. Second: does not arise." Jacqueline understood that Williams was in love with her and disgusted with himself. "Michael gives me terrible little presents for Christmas," she said, "all that sort of thing; I wouldn't care if... but I went out for the day, and was not back the following night, and he was just – you know, very curt; I mean, am I supposed... He said, 'Oh, you were away for the week?' I said, 'Oh, I come and go.'"

Jacqueline became younger and noisier; Williams's handkerchiefs were her home; unhurriedly, on holiday and walking at home in the hottest summer, her limbs in an indolent pattern, she assisted the old man in his work. "I will give what help, as I have said." Jacqueline's presence distracted him; Williams looked older, stooped; he said he had never intended taking her into his office – he could not concentrate – he blamed her. She offered him coffee every thirty minutes from a device which sent a column of water into the air. For a minute he waited for the necessary response: it would not be recalled.

Jacqueline spoke to her husband. "I thought let's contact your father again and see. I had this idea which might be acceptable... but no. Not that I like him, but he lives on his own. I thought I might – he might be rather stimulating, but he's like a sensitive child; you don't see him – you don't know how your father's changed. Almost tearful. I speak to him – he likes listening; understanding smiles come to his face. But I would not have him back if he were dying." "You're not keen to become involved," Michael said. "It's not that."

Michael sacked several key men. "I was born with an unlucky face," one said. Michael bent down, examined the nose and cheekbone; the eyes came round large without speaking. The factory was an excellent place – a welcoming place – in the circumstances, very fine. The man would be pleased if they would let him stay. Two others were sacked; they started a business raising hamsters for medical research. One was permitted to stay. He underwent the routine checks; the blood count was normal. A wonderful place. The lucky man said it was wonderful: an island with a corrugated roof; plenty to eat; a family of lovely people.

Chapter 11

WILLIAMS CAME in answer to Michael's bell. "Do sit down." The chair was deep, soft, easily adjustable to suit people of different shapes – heavy lobes of foam rubber, strengthened internally with pliable steel. "There's nothing wrong with my work?" "I had to be sure," Michael said; "I did not want to trouble you." The vacant face had not heard. "In a few years perhaps..." Williams began. "I'll hear no more of that." The son's eyes were empty. "Well, well, it's time for my nap." Williams went to his room and lay down; the blankets stretched the length of the body, from the scraps of hair to the wrists, his head bent as Jacqueline tucked in another strip of blanket; his son said nothing – Michael watched his wife's hands from a distance while the operation was completed.

The morning rains were green across the hills; the trees would begin to bloom in five minutes. Williams could see one quarter of the black door at the end of the corridor. Michael began his tour of other men's work: he conferred with managers, was absent to all of inferior rank. Williams became concerned lest he be shifted from his office. "The size of a man's desk can be crucial." He arranged to eat and sleep in his office and moved in the necessary furniture; he called it "the cage", or "my fourteen-by-twelve".

Sometimes Williams talked with intelligence, but most of his time was spent in his little room, dressing and undressing with care, bustling about with fantastic energy, folding his elegant possessions, arranging and rearranging his collections of private papers, his memoirs, his revelations, slowly perfecting his life.

Each morning Jacqueline tidied Williams's papers and cleaned his room; he would allow no one else to do it. He talked to her as she swept the small moist room. "It's got the length, but I need it about four feet wider. I keep forgetting as I go in the door – the cooker is at the side. There's grooves to fit the table in, if you want. Last night I had to move to one of the bunks – I had pains in my back the whole night; it wasn't a soft joint – it was a spine. So here I am, lying down, exactly this width, and on that side I've got the built-in cupboard – I should think it's about five foot six; I slid, I banged my feet against it – it's only plywood; I tucked everything in all along the bottom; my son says two people could sleep here – but that's the double one with the joint; this is the single; I've had to move from the double to the single. I've not measured the ceiling height; I should think it's four or five inches above my head; it makes the whole place steaming – all the moisture, you see – it steams up as soon as you have the heat on; it's shocking. My bed's too warm, so you know what I do? I put my damp things on the pipes. And this miserable business of water; I can't have my breakfast in peace, in my dressing gown – I have to get all dressed up and walk and get the water; you bring this lot here, you wash yourself, you bring all this lot back again – you need a huge kettle really – one of those enormous things. All I do in the morning is I do some toast." Jacqueline was required to listen and nod, then to stand by the window, look down at the beds of flowers and admire the view.

Williams clung tenaciously to his remaining privileges, his unique uniform. To his father's complaints of neglect, Michael replied, "It seems to me that you have not lost, but gained a family" – indicating himself, Jacqueline, the managers who accompanied him on his morning tour. Williams said he was stiff from lying around – rusty – the food was too rich, the day's work too short to justify keeping in trim; he was unused to the day without work. He complained of sounds in the ceiling – tramping feet, furniture being moved. Williams had his room soundproofed, with padded walls and ceiling. "Thwack!" A wet mop threw a stream of dirty water under the door. "More than I can bear" – staring in the mirror at his great thick face.

The firm's name was changed, coinciding with fresh activity; from side to side with constant increase in intensity when attempts were made in certain directions, usually upwards, success was achieved. There was always some movement forcibly in one direction, and an attempt to maintain it for a length of time in what corresponded to the boundaries of action. It paralysed when driven in the wrong direction at a time when it would otherwise be strong. The growth was imperfect; centres of power appeared, but of them little was known; there were changes in these centres – altered states brought about by abnormal conditions; their course was not clear.

From this point a growing rebellion was observed in Williams. He lay awake till after midnight, pencilling notes on scraps of paper. He was found with confidential memoranda in his possession. These were the early signs. Michael followed these symptoms, which closely concerned him.

Papers which fell on the floor or were found in Williams's wastepaper basket were taken secretly by Jacqueline to Michael's office, where he laid them on his desk and tried to piece them together. Michael noted the times his name occurred; invariably the only name was Williams; the notes consisted mainly of reports on the alleged inadequacies of the junior clerical staff.

Michael talked of "mischief-makers in our ranks", and advocated "measures to counteract the spread of misinformation". "We all know," he said, "those noisy types, full of complaints but short of solutions, who think that what they lack in force of argument can be made good by the cunning of its presentation. It will pay dividends to combat subversive influences who thrive in times of difficulty and make the task of their superiors immeasurably more anxious, but who would not survive for a moment if the real truth were known." Michael's intelligence was plain, but his arrogance began to defeat him. His position was precarious; at any time the board could demand his resignation. Michael was not unaware of this possibility, nor was it intended that he should be. It was impossible to remove all traces of the old ways and the old name; on the other hand, "It must be done".

On transfer from the executive to the clerical department, it was customary to take leave of one's chief before the removal of desk and papers, but Williams omitted this ritual. He said he had called on Michael but had found him out. This deceived no one; the protest achieved its purpose. Williams left his papers with Jacqueline; the notes and reports filled thirty boxes. The form of Williams's new work was decided for him. He would not take a clerical job until he was assured that he would be awarded a substantial pension – then he accepted without question. Jacqueline accompanied him to the lift; he waved goodbye; he went down to the basement, where the typists worked. A woman took him in charge and entered his name – one among four hundred. There were seven to a room; he had his own table and chair.

"I was away from the office for six months. When I returned, there was no suitable opening, so I came here." Williams talked to the man laying carpet in his room; he knew how to handle him. He boasted of the position he had once enjoyed; he had no need to keep up appearances – he drank and sang, he acted freely; only his notes remained secret. Michael let things take their course; then a stop was put to the private writings. Williams's pencils and paper were confiscated. The old man had difficulty in becoming obedient; he was discovered scribbling secretly at night: "This needs nerve." Williams confided in Jacqueline his method of concealing his "last words"; he pointed with his foot at the floorboard under which his papers were hidden. She knew the strain across his throat, the neck, his face stiff with ugliness, the mouth hidden behind obscure papers. She agreed to supply Williams with the firm's headed notepaper; she left him a message to this effect, the vital words underlined. She could not give him all the details, but a hint would be given if a hint were needed. "I talk to Michael maybe twice a week; he'll never tell me anything now. I know there are several deals pending, but I don't really know; his office is a difficult place for me to go to now. There's been all sorts of troubles; actually, I'll tell you a secret – not about me, about Michael – ha ha, very funny: he meets a girl, in a hotel, actually, just round the corner – they have terrific rows, actually." "Where?"

"Round the corner – now don't spoil it – you know what he's like. I used to complain in my childish way, but everything was so hopeless; I suppose certain types shut out the external world completely," Jacqueline said. "I should have thought there were two kinds," Williams said. "I was thinking of really crazy old men."

Williams asked for a private room where he could write, but however hard he worked, he failed; he was no worker. He was moved by love of the absurd, in order to justify and preserve his individuality; this taste became a disease: it took root – he could not disregard it.

Again Williams was transferred; the policy was to keep him on the move: stop him settling down and learning enough to make himself useful, to prevent him influencing others. He ignored the fresh instructions; they did not concern him. Another clerk took over Williams's vacated table, as the old man was given nothing to do. "I came here to do a job," Williams said. "You've got the job." Then Jacqueline came to tell him: "Everyone is being moved from here, from this corridor." Williams grabbed her hard; his reaction was to kiss – he began to; persisted. "Now don't try that. This moving around will be finished in time. Michael has his reasons for his decisions. He's sending you and two others, the three of you, back to the old building. It will be more convenient, more spacious; everything will be easier, more familiar; there's nothing for you to do here. You need not see Michael; I spent the whole night arguing with him. Everything you need is on the way. All he asks is that you go with as little fuss as possible," she said. "Michael told you to tell me – to persuade me to go. It's no use, I won't go," Williams said. "It's too late to object now."

When he was taken into the new department, Williams had a different table; it was a change – he and the change embraced – there was no proof of victimization. Yet as he unpacked his things, the mouth drooped – the same shade of brown as the boots and trousers. Williams's mood would not change; he drank the last of the flask of whisky. It was good – nothing so good. He had now to sign the deed of transfer. "We need your signature on this line, right here." "What is the sense? I can sign ten thousand lines." Jacqueline smiled. "Calm down. Have a drink." Williams began to peel the label off the whisky bottle; he said he felt fine. "Oh yes, it's funny, because this new chief clerk – I'd heard a lot about him from the others, but I didn't know what to expect. I didn't go straight into his office, which was just as well because I walked into him – it was rather a shock. I've never known an office like this; it's the worst ever – it's never light, is it? Yesterday was worse; it was dull – admittedly it was raining, but it was dull. You know, the funny thing is – this is strange now – when I was on the road and slept in my car, I didn't feel shut in; I could sit in the dark in my car and feel all right, but in this place I feel shut in. It would be nice to do something about it, but what can you do?"

Williams took his transfer form to the personnel office, where deeds of transfer converged and were registered. The form made the move official if it was brought by hand with the transferee's signature affixed. The typewriters took over in a frenzy of activity; what little time remained was concentrated in the typists' room. They raised the question of Williams's table. "Who usually supplies the table?" They looked to him; it was his responsibility. Williams had played this game before – as accomplice, rather than victim. The cleaners were dusting and blowing the dust around him as the paper was angled at a dozen different angles past three. After an hour's probe into the form's validity, the cleaners were assembled outside; they looked embarrassed; each suggested an experience he had been denied. The matter was to be decided. Williams sighed like a man turning over in bed, and he said he hoped his judges would not prove amateurs. His mind diagnosed a burst of sound; the clerk stared from his chair: "Who said that? Was it you? Are you mad?" Gagged by the other's voice, Williams's eyes blinked in his head: "Hard to say – no, I don't think so" – a small dry voice, not his own, "I might have been in error." The clerk with the pen said, "There may be a short delay – no more." They blindfolded him and turned him round many times, lay him across a desk in a room on his own.

The dullness in the new room – the tortured boredom; Williams examined his pencil on the desk, held it up in the air, fingered it, ran his nail halfway down, picked at the soft wood. "Jacqueline said I should calm down – well, it's calm enough here." It was quiet. "I'm a fighter by nature – I've always had to fight – mind you, it's not been easy. I'm an incurable optimist. I don't like planning too far ahead." Clustered around the small window were a dozen birds; someone had thrown bread on the sill. The birds tried to get into the room; one flew at the window and tapped its beak against the glass. The voice of a stranger told him to sit down, and the excitement ended. "Time to get out, fast." Williams closed his eyes and turned crafty with a thought a thousand miles away. "Pull yourself together." He crossed to the door, where someone waited curiously with a sharp push to return him to his room.

Chapter 12

THOUGH HIS MUSCLES informed him of life like a vice, Williams was not sure; he became aware of a deterioration; he had learnt the Latin name, but everyone explained the thing differently, confused him to the point of exasperation; one said the word referred to one thing, another to another – the contradictions drove him mad. On his own, the high ceiling was silent, the mind wandered, he felt easier. They were discussing him again; they had a taste for disease, whose names slipped in from the remote land of Rome; these names were men in his room. Williams's son had scrubbed hands – Michael's hand against the desk – the desk had nothing to complain of; the nails were clean. Michael's tie was grey, but the eyes talked; it was unnatural – the curious eyes were unhappy, neither gold nor blue, but grey, an extinction of colour like a long day of rain.

The pains in his body compelled Williams to seek an explanation of their different causes. He enjoyed the pain's intensity, but asked for pills to kill his will to struggle for the remnants of his life. His son insisted he maintain the fight, warned him against the crime against oneself. In the battle between them, the stronger supported the weaker; one lay still on a narrow shelf, the other held him there. The son attempted to exchange roles, to submit. Michael never appreciated the older man, nor approached the person. The weak body of the infirm man was his weapon. Instead of widening, Williams narrowed, reduced to the strictest limits; the son was forced to submit under the threat of the father's succumbing. Their existence remained based on mutual extermination – the son supported by fact, the father by his primitive spirit, the one dominated by intelligence; but of greater importance were Williams's habits and character, his enjoyment of life against Michael's wasting energy. The old man developed his ideas, and a few months before his death Michael placed a bandage over his mouth, telling him that it was Williams himself who had insisted on the pitiless struggle, and that it was in his father's own interests that he should attempt to forget his existence.

Instantly, Williams recalled his function and became part of it. He dumped his case on the desk. He looked from the window at the few trees that still grew on the bar of green; his serenity returned. He read the papers and thought: "If I had not read that before, it would be interesting." He grew fussy about his food: "I will not eat another meat pie." He stepped out of the front door to meet the sun; he took off his coat and was blown over by the wind. He had his monthly medical examination and made a note: in fine shape. Old age was a trick after too many drinks. "It's ridiculous," he said next morning, when he was refused a second helping; the food was good; he had bathed before breakfast, he was enjoying himself. Up and looking for love: there had never been a more heated eye, none more magnificent than the moment he said "Look at that girl!", walked into town and sat through the nightly movie, found himself a girl nearly twice life-size, bestowed on her the favours of an emperor.

With work a necessity, the night filled with thick writing; the accusations accumulated; the result compressed into a line. These were Williams's best hours; the cracks in the wall blew warmth into the room; he sat at his desk, papers on a tray, tapping the tray with a pencil. "It will mean power." He smiled through the smoke at the bottle of ink which would not keep quiet. His final report was to be complete, the last draft done in the course of the summer. A thorough examination of work methods would be ordered; certain facts would emerge, the existence of which had not been suspected. The board would learn the name of the author of the third anonymous report – it had been kept from them; now they would meet face to face. As Williams prepared for the crucial meeting, Jacqueline stood by the door, staring at water trickling over the wooden desk – he had knocked over a glass of water. He whipped his papers out of the way, and lay them on blotting paper. Her face had the appearance of wax. His fifty boxes of notes were wheeled away on a trolley. He put on his best clothes and asked her if he was "fit to be seen by people who had ceased to exist". She said she would wait for him; he must remember who he was; he had a good memory. She would stay and look after his papers; she sorted them into neat piles.

The tea-break hooter sounded; the scramble for cups and biscuits began. A woman wheeling a tea trolley barged into Williams scurrying down the corridor; he apologized and offered her a cigarette. A nose was picked before the pouring of tea; two packets of tea were stuck together by chewing gum. Some tea spilt over his shoes; he bent down to wipe them with his handkerchief.

"How did you get on?" Jacqueline asked. "You know," Williams said, "I'm better off here. I could not face the winter in your place – the size of the electric bill; me, I don't mind where I am; I must say there's something I like about this little room – cosy – the construction is warmer in winter." "It's a war, and you've lost," she said. "I've a good mind to invite myself over to your place for the warmth – just call round and say, 'I'm freezing – could you spare some fire?'" "Did you speak to Michael?" "I had nothing to say to him," Williams replied. "I must get home and prepare his meal," she said. "You could stay here – sleep in this room – if you don't mind getting up in the dark and leaving before morning." Jacqueline did not blame him, but it was too depressing.

By winter Williams realized that the length of his report was inconvenient – he could not complete the work; it capsized; it was a mass of blots; lack of time was the reason. He studied the single sheet of paper – the parallel lines had a subtle meaning. The twelve involved paragraphs had marked his face; the muddled sentences revealed the strain. "Come along now, time to stop." Jacqueline tidied his papers. "What of my research? I need to question Michael, to know what was in his mind." "Don't worry him, he's busy." "I don't need him – there are others – I have often talked with angels on the subject." "Oh... how dreadful." She was crying – with triumph. Williams remembered each detail – papers lost, pages rewritten. The day he had had it right, there had been an outburst from her. "That day I was inspired," he said. "What an amateur you were! And every year you celebrate the anniversary!" "I am writing the history of the world. A new Bible." "I'm not a complete fool." She had whispered like a murderer: "The words are in disorder – there is no sense; you are not in the mood." She had not come out with it – she had hinted, spoken without vibration, with the intention of being inaudible, "No, that is not it; it needs to be changed." When the work had gone well she had looked unhappy, shown alarm; it had been a revelation, her reaction, her face, all those years – three years, at least – like the smell of his mother's arms; he'd been a fool; he could not hold that against her.

Jacqueline blushed when Williams asked her if she had arrived by car; he said he did not need her to wipe the sweat off his face – her hands were clammy – he had seen the lights of their car, the glints of sequins on her dress, the full skirt sweeping the floor. She would not take off her coat; she chatted about the crash – the front wing dented by a bus; the silk-dressed Daimler smiled politely; the driver would not let them go; he had grabbed the wheel; Michael had called the police – that had calmed them down soon enough. Between them, the narrow gap, a sleeping bird disclosed, desk of wood, a filthy comb. "Well?" Jacqueline asked. Around her lurked the smell of dignity as she crossed the room to ask questions; she had married a kidney-shaped object; the shops were full of good things; forty million shopkeepers were short of silver – their appeal for funds must not go unanswered. Jacqueline made allowances, disregarded the dirt; there was no call to be rude. She asked the name of the nurse who had let her in. Williams's mouth stretched over the question. "What was wrong with that girl – she was so rude?" Jacqueline asked. His lips rubbed slowly against each other. "Nothing wrong with her; she was in trouble in the factory. I have tried to help her – she was badly treated. I help all I can." "You're not well. I have discussed it with Michael; you must take care – try to forget what you were; spend more time in sleep – a small thing can knock you off balance." Jacqueline continued with a detective's calm; Williams looked impatiently from the powder on her nose to the hands tied together in prayer. "I could order you out." Jacqueline opened the door to go; the nurse bustled in with three cups of tea on a tray. "Now what's going on? This won't do. He must not get overexcited." The two women looked at the sweating face above the piles of papers. He had two nurses, a girl and a woman, both angry because he could not hold the cup steady – it had something to do with the central nervous system – shouting at the sick man who spilt the hot tea. Williams asked what had become of the parcels sent by his son; the sugar had been "mislaid" – there was no sugar for his tea. Jacqueline said he should not complain – he was living in comparative comfort – she wondered why he chose this, of all times, to worry about food. His sores were spreading – he was dying, drinking the bitter tea.

"Nice legs," he said of the nurse, when she had taken the cups back to the kitchens. They heard the sound of smashed dishes. "How are you getting on down there?" he called after her. She had held him all morning; when she had gone, with force detached from the desk, she had held out her hand to him. "Would you have done the same?" he asked Jacqueline. He pulled some folders from a drawer; the girl bent over him to shift some books to make room for the folders – soft contours, two low hills in her blouse. "Thank you, my dear." Jacqueline pulled a crumpled piece of paper from one of the files. "With your permission" – she smoothed the paper on her lap to decipher the hurried writing. "Will you come tomorrow?" he asked her. "I couldn't say." The drawn curtain sighed with rain; Jacqueline patted the back of his chair, her clean hands close to his face.

"I offer you freedom; why not take it?" Williams spoke to the lamp on his desk. Jacqueline's high voice passed over. "You stay because you hate," he said. "Of the three – perhaps four – of us, you are the one who knows what to do." Williams sniffed the tea, gave the biscuits to the nurse, who ate anything; he was tempted by the smell of chocolate, but he deprived himself; he watched the girl eat. In a corner of his room, he found a spider for company, and fell in love with it; he confided the story of his life. Now he owned his home; he had it from God, whose face was cleaner than a clock. The radio instructed the people: "Follow my leader!" He sang submissively.

A man in a hat walked into the room; his fashionable cigar floated in front like a gun; Michael, and with him the inevitable lady moving like a man. Williams was caught; in place of a meal gladly offered, his son had dragged him away from the food. Williams spilt soup over his desk; he touched the bread with his fingers; his back pressed against the chair to prevent himself from being taken. Outside, winter froze to death in the street, it broke the windows; thirty frozen people were produced in evidence; smashed machines lay instead of food upon the tables. The colour of Williams's clothes remained unchanged; his report was not complete. His son Michael had read the first part – he had said the humour was splendid, but apart from that he did not like it; his son had passed him in the corridor. The dud torch and the homeless girl coughed behind the screen; it was the fog – a space filled with ersatz lavender – while thieves made easy money in the south.

The nurse smiled at Jacqueline. "May I treat you as a friend?" This attitude the older woman found disturbing; the rare word "friend" used as a greeting by this young woman of inferior rank – no more than a servant – it was annoying. "I have nothing to say to you." Jacqueline was exquisitely dressed, her blouse in fashionable scarlet. "My time is taken up with this poor invalid." Jacqueline spoke grandly, proud and rich, her husband a person of importance. Her politeness appeared as disguise for her suffering; her calmness impressed for a time. Sharing the tiny room, she seated herself on Williams's lap, an excuse for a flickering line; he described his gift for catching fish at sea; the fire blazed through force of habit – it could not be pretended; they let it burn itself out: the stale old man and the overflowering wife; the handling of meat and money. Williams smiled like a child; Jacqueline drank her cup of tea; as she named God, her face became sad. Williams asked, "How do I know I have not died in the night, been reborn and given a history and previous life and set of memories to complete the new life given? Do I die each night, and born again by morning?" She did not respond – sat as if she could not hear him. She turned to the girl – white socks and red hair; her factory uniform had her badge of rank on the breast. "Do you know that you are beautiful?" Jacqueline said. "I can't help it," the girl replied. "I am serious." "It's all the same to me." "My husband could help you transform your life." "He's your husband, not mine – it can't be helped." The woman inclined her head, considered. The girl asked, "Is he really all that rich?" "I would prefer not to discuss it." It had been a wooing across the valley. "Since you give me no sign I shall not try again." The girl understood that her chance had come and gone; she got up and behaved as if she had not heard the curt reply. Jacqueline spoke to Williams about his health, and her impatience showed. The nurse sat by herself in the corner of the small room; she knew the man would die; the plump young girl sat crying. Jacqueline glanced at the sobbing nurse; her shortness and peculiar mouth did not become her. "It was good of you to come, but you cannot help; leave now, he is tired."

When Williams said he must do something useful, they gave him work – it was good for him. It was cardboard laid flat, and on one side he stuck cellophane. It was not easy – sometimes he bent the cardboard back to make a box.

Michael and Jacqueline discussed the family problem. "It seems he was transferred to a smaller room," Jacqueline said. "Some people said he rather resented it; they just automatically, it seems, made a decision, to make feeding him easier, you see; he didn't want that – none of us wanted it – but what can you do?" "It's in your hands entirely," Michael said. "He's still very shaky, very much so, but improving. I'll always remember him: he had a man's face, then he was broken up; one moment he was a man, then a heap of junk. He was someone I thought I knew, and then absolutely mad – he is, they say he is, and he's not terribly good at tests, the record shows. It's amazing how a person can influence you; I used to respect him immensely, and when I got to know him, he was already ill, you know?" "Embarrassing," Michael said. "Well, I didn't let myself be embarrassed, so it wasn't too bad. I had to meet this new female – you know, you get the type, a girl who knows what's what," Jacqueline said. "I don't know much about her." "He had a sort of magic," she said. "Yes," Michael agreed; "he could be most exciting." "Well, I saw him with this new girl in his room, and then – most extraordinary thing – they were kissing. She had a shock of auburn hair down here, which didn't look too terribly dyed. Your father has changed – he might have been a Swiss from the sort of restraint," she said. "I'll go down and see him. It is only a question of finding the time," Michael said. "The last time I saw him," Jacqueline said, "as soon as I arrived, he said I had to divorce my husband for him, leave your flat and God knows what; he had his reasons – he talked at great length, you know, about me, and you, and his life and how it all happened; he talked and talked and I couldn't say a word – he was half manic." "Using the word in the sense of the manic side of the depressive state?" "This voice came from the chair – I mean, honestly, when you talk about mad, that man was. He once had all sorts of abilities; he's the kind of person who never stops for a minute; you can never kind of… I was impressed far beyond – one minute absolute bursting and floods of tears." "I had a dose of that," Michael said. "And the next minute there was very little wrong with him." "You mean there was very little visibly wrong with him?" "But I couldn't stay – it's natural I couldn't," Jacqueline said. "Now you can get back on your feet again," Michael said. "I write to him every day; he said he was going to send all letters back, so I went on just the same; there's nothing to write – I can't lie, but I write." "One part of him is irrational – nothing can break through," Michael said. "There's no argument. I always said it was on purpose – that side of him is completely… you can't break through – have you noticed how much I am affected? It affects me; you can't expect anything else," she said. "My feeling is forget the whole thing," Michael said. "That's right – I keep telling myself – there are signs, in the whole face; there is something – I don't know."

Chapter 13

THE FOOD TROLLEY was pushed from Williams's room: an untouched chicken on a plate, narrow and breathless; a piece of grey cheese with a thumb-print on it. Jacqueline was nice and clean; she pushed the trolley smoothly over the rubberized floor to the room where Michael, his tweed coat flecked with green, held the door by its chromium ring. He said she had kept him hanging around for twenty minutes. She stared and said nothing. Michael winked and said, "Which meal is this?" "I don't know." "You'll have to take it back. We can't afford to waste good food."

Jacqueline shuffled her feet constantly at night; Williams thought her feet had a life independent from her body. In the corner, a pointed cross: she stood in front of it. The doctor walked in unhurriedly, balanced himself easily, halted. Their palms touched in a universal gesture of "you know what I want". Jacqueline glanced down; he pushed her lightly; her eyes clicked shut; the second step back, soft-footed against the wall; again the click of empty eyes, Williams heard loud, indifferently. The doctor walked back to the door. "Go home and wait; I'll come." Williams looked from his bed at the snakes in her hair, the eyes harsh, different from home, walls made of bricks topped by whitened wood, beneath the wall a path of earth and stones; the blankets were yellow, the beds low; he leant away to avoid seeing them. Cautiously he felt the outlines of his face. He had a body with appendages, legs – a convenient if simplified form of locomotion. One appendage was the head; the function of this organ had yet to be determined; it was decorated with bristles.

"I missed it in the dark. They're trying to make me miss the best meal of the day," Williams said. "They say it's best to stop all food," Jacqueline replied. A hot spider landed on his eye. It was two paces to the door, and Williams started towards it; he came up fast from the floor in a panic; he knew where he was – he was here for a short stay. He lifted himself and pushed out, turning his head for help; the narrow wrist hesitated a yard away. His midday meal in a swinging pot was bobbing towards him, held on a string by someone laughing, fiddling with a wireless set.

"I enjoy all the crazy things I used to do," Williams talked to Michael; "I've got the same energy I always had. People are so kind – that's why I want to get back and meet more people; I like people; I'm always doing something – I come and go – that's what is so wonderful. I am going on – oh dear, some people get like that; I should be settling down, but I still enjoy myself; I can go all old school tie – it puts the gleam back into any woman's eye." He was out of bed and talking to himself, his body hidden by the open door.

By craning her head round the door, Jacqueline got sight of him; she grabbed his legs and tugged him towards the bed; he seemed to shrink; a moment later the kneeling woman got up; she smiled; the grey man was in bed.

Williams had no more worry; he leant towards sleep, preferred to be cared for; they were not murderers, nor would they let him go. The light steadied, died. Moving without friction, without anger, the big-wheeled trolley whizzed easily enough, lifted, clanged, went whistling over the floor. A bandage was taken away, dropped in a bin. The bruise in the centre of the sky formed and spread; the night, without being told that it must be quiet, was quiet; the furious and mortified blaming monkeys slept. The first Williams had known of heavy sleep was ushered in; his body hung from poles; he was unable to plan; it was no one's fault. An unlit globe hung over him till the night ended. Nurse checked the window: the lock was intact; she walked from window to window.

Woken by a sharp light impossible to avoid, he waited for nurse, who moved ahead of him a distance of inches. The trees outside were the things he had failed to do. Confined in bed, Jacqueline held him there to stop him injuring himself. Like others in beds below, Williams had begun the year with his mouth on hers, taken his life from her. She had improved as a killer – inventive, meticulous, systematic, painstaking, capable of thought; she could sneak and shoot in the back. She was a lethal plaything, religious violinist, destroyer. He spoke to her. "It's lovely here – you get used to it;

persuade Michael to come down; turn the mattress, just get me the papers; get Michael to come – ask him by letter – he must have a holiday too; lovely here, isn't it – phone him, otherwise he will be too late." "Goodnight," she said. "Goodnight. It's warm." "Hm?" "Warm. When you come in. I mean, I'd like to go to London with you. Like. Might. Do. What you do. Listen, I bought these pyjamas for a fiver – listen – and when they wear out I throw them away and buy another pair."

In bed, the perfect place of ambush, between restless neighbours who tempted him into uncomplicated suicide, Williams acknowledged flickered visions of expert self-slaughter. He considered the problem. He lived in exile, in the bowels of another creature. He had food. He could not eat; he did not need to eat. He had no means. There was no development, nothing startling in his life. Though he was cooped up, he led a complete life; he was capable of limited movement. He could anchor himself in position. He had weight, which protected him from being dislodged. He was bathed in soup. He breathed by habit. He possessed a mouth, the centre of alarm, close to the spine and the stomach; the mouth moved – fingers across the lips, steady, tired at last; the fascination of the thin strands of pain still held him, relaxed, compelled to give in and wrap his arms around his body.

Williams was recovering on schedule; he had had a comfortable night; the mild sedation had been dispensed with; he had walked round his room, taking several steps unaided. He had taken small amounts of soft food by mouth. His family had visited him, and they had discussed a wide range of subjects of mutual interest.

With her mouth Jacqueline covered the sore on his neck – no smile, a cool animal with soothing pastes, her face bound with strips of cotton.

He wanted no food but sleep; he slept like a sickness; the heaviness rested on the floor; the best he could do was sleep, the mouth full of water – better off in every way. The sea of gravel moved and swelled without water and was never still – a marvellous sea of stones and trees that no man could cross.

* * *

He could see the car racing past the scene – it was effective, it was likely to be seen – and the fatal accident – the marks on the road where the wheels would come off. The technique they planned to use in that particular case included radio contact between driver and police to let them know what was going on. It was simple for the driver to operate: "We live with what can be used in evidence, and we have for years." The elderly body with the big stomach was found in the stationary car: knees apart, holding on to himself. It was frightful. It had given him no pleasure to watch the passers-by. It was necessary to tow away the car, put out its lights; it had been left in a precarious place. Everything had to be taken from it – the key, the licence, the luggage. The body, which had squeezed itself into the small car, had to be watched for hours so that no one should steal it, while the flesh was softening. The man had no money. He had been preoccupied with business. On his seventieth birthday he had found a way out. Came the evening when he carelessly left himself out in the cold; he was quite chilled; he crouched in the back of the empty car. In the street there were few people; he had not begun – it was unfair; life had gone badly – he had begun and ended.

Chapter 14

THE THIRD DAY of hot water admitted a remote possibility; the quiet was a holiday in a garden; the body of the father was in the quiet house three times a day; the physical family disappearing. The collapse of the lips, fumes from the cracks in the walls, the head of ice in the fatal air, the green watch stopped at one.

Michael took the gas-mask form of public transport – the horse on the point of collapse, the frightening white cotton, a series of paralytic gutters, crosses across the world, the stretched arms of women, the precipice across her shoulders, the lush women swaying on bare feet, the hard remote region, sacking placed over the land, thighs raw in the wooden box; the tall thin man became aggressive, the neck swollen and dangerous, the drunken heads in the wild country; the white mud became slow, the shirt at one o'clock was sixty-five years old, with only an hour of daylight left for the unconvicted murderer.

The question staggered under the weight of the question. Michael was asked for half an hour. The queues of flowers moved towards the day. How much would he pay for a single chair? The day for ten days consisted of a box on a table. The rubber boots were lost. The crying blowing kisses booming, the foretaste of bruises and bitterness, continually bombarded by bombs the size and shape of God, the taste of earth tomorrow.

The worldly estate had been divided: there was some suspicion that Williams had planned to donate everything to a foundation to benefit every person continuously employed in the factory during a period of five years before his death. Fifty boxes of banknotes were said to have been found in his room, concealed by timber, the paper money wrapped in cloth. These rumours, in an hour, brought two hundred to his bed; then eleven hundred workers gathered below the windows, with Michael's permission, to witness the dispositions. Michael and his wife Jacqueline were neutral – neither could be regarded as belonging to any faction or being interested in the outcome of any dispute about the will. They had hardly known the old chap – they had kept in touch – they were three who met at Christmas. The old man had apparently wished to draw attention to the family situation; the frustration of this posthumous desire, however, was the purpose of Michael's presence; he was tense and watchful – it was, after all, a pitiful, curious business – and Michael, on his voyage through the world, would have avoided this chair most gratefully – not that in some measure he would not have appreciated a small present. Michael had been in a similar situation before: he had had a present from his wife's father, who had had a certain dream, and again, as the one who attended the dying, Michael had taken the customary gift from a boy who had passed away some years ago – his young companion; there had been a watch in his pocket and a wallet now empty; nothing dishonest about emptying the pockets of the dead – robbing the coffin before the body was cold. Michael hoped the sequence would not be repeated, nor the dreams from his unconscious in which he walked close to a man in a shower of stones: each held a net and a sack. For two days Michael remained in his room, listening, waving his arms above his head. He had proved that he had not profited from the dying sense of gratitude; he had not wanted survival for himself – it was like food pushed down the throat.

Michael was compelled to retain in his office the official portrait of the founder of the firm. He wanted to take it off its hook. He touched his father's painted face; it had been struck by lightning. He changed the position of his desk; the portrait remained for a purpose. The image was visual. Hard to explain the memory of the old man holding a bottle, the cold from the broken window, someone wrapping him up. Jacqueline's high voice stretched from the window to the street. Michael returned to the portrait; the painter had been poor in terms of line and tone; the background was white to suggest light. From Michael's window: the glass-covered yellowish day; sheep floated downriver; a thousand priests sold shaving soap; a ship glided down a filmed canal; two men stood by a lamp; the street came to an end. His father had been a difficult subject; the smell of oil paint had offended him. "You know me well enough," he had said, too tired to lose his temper.

Michael wrapped his night blanket tight again. He had to be sure – he had been sure last Sunday at the death. Go back there again? His hands clenched in the corridor incredulously. Then, "For Christ's sake!" at something on the pavement.

Michael attended to money matters – he studied the glass box of copper coin, the marble cheeks of the girl cashier; a cigarette in the thick moustache – the cigarette irritated her; he strolled back to the banknotes lying on the counter like herrings on a slab, the cold finger along the cigarette into the mess as the hard boy went forwards. She watched the shillings and pence. "Come downstairs" – the heavy cash register strained at the implications. "And supposing someone comes along?" The second death made the same story – the man in the café, the woman sweeping crumbs from the table.

The second shock helped to pinpoint the happy pair, to make their life appear lucky. The public pressure of malicious gossip increased. The accuser rose from his place. Michael had mentioned the will five times to five persons, and what had that to do with it? The formal plea was heard. "Let us look at those occasions – the previous lies exposed." It was not yet time for the truth. "I'm sorry, you must wait." While they waited, the corpse went by in a box, originally painted white, now overlaid with various colours; the black and gold moved down and staggered away. Michael whistled through the gap in his teeth; he was honest, sincere, liberal – he knew enough about history: "Here Is a Message" booming through the more than that.

"A split family liberates energy like a split atom." Michael said he could make no progress: he would leave; go north. He made his statement to the press, with black coffee, black tie. "After the funeral I'll leave town – I'll take nothing; a man on a donkey; a thousand miles with a piece of string; I'll set up as a monk." No newspaper gave a fair account of what he had said: "Son leaves business. He gets out on his own".

Michael crossed the street; the railings, the drop to the basement. The street paused; the eye was painted on the wall of the house. A gate in a green light; the ground sloped upwards; the main road smelt of mud; the steady road curved towards a new element of power. The sky was crowded with stars unrolling, hunted, agitated. Going to his retreat in the country, Michael made to lie there. Who may sleep here? Anyone. No one is asked his name. No one is asked his occupation or his past. Night lodgers are given bed, coffee, free of charge. In the morning they receive coffee and bread. They are then free to go away. The sole condition is that they take part in evening and morning prayers and make a contribution of twenty guineas a week. Michael said his father was rich; they thought he was talking about some other. The next day he left; the thing was over; he began to cover his tracks. A red flag signalled the train out; chaos splashed from the jungle: apocalypse, mysticism, prophecy, blood in enamel bowls. He turned for a last look. The wall below the cemetery was blotted from sight by the cold wind. The moon was surprised at nothing; she thought the earth was one of her puppies.

A prominent businessman affected by travelling overnight broke his journey in bizarre circumstances during his tour of the north yesterday... while his wife today in his home... the couple were on their way... his sacrifice outside Perth in the line of duty, to attend the funeral of his father, the christening of fame and medals. Michael became confused by the twisting bends, and part of a bridge collapsed onto a hospital. His wife assisted; she went with him – "I gave what help, as I have said." Their Jaguar lay out of action for an hour, because the suitcase failed; the coffee in flasks was kept in evidence; there was only one driver.

Michael waved and wept in a hotel room, lolling about on a low-level lie-down for extra comfort; the guests in open-necked shirts sat next to the hot water pipes, responded to the tension he generated. He was himself on the bonfire; he kissed God's sinewy arse; his ankles felt the cat.

His father's hands showed brick-red beneath the white cane chair; the portrayed line across the eyes, the blanket over the glass table – as if a child had given the table a kick and gone to sleep. The room put a bullet through him; the young man's teeth counted the years; the confusion of a choice to be made by the one who survived, climbed, recognized time written on walls, accounts for the eye to study. A collector of art, Michael was struck by the sinister implications of a message which described an event which had not yet taken place; he caught sight of someone across the room and remained quiet, arms folded.

Chapter 15

R ECOVERED FROM BEING ATTACKED by bees, Michael arrived back from his country home in time for the funeral. He was told that everyone was talking; Williams's trouble had been his sons, the factory, the brothels; like a huge Italian drowned in wine, the tall, tangled man had fallen through burning floors, stunned by the loss of his child. Jacqueline said she was "dried up"; she "felt no sense of victory".

Michael was taken on a tour of the funeral route; the splendid monuments were pointed out; no less than two hundred possibilities as to the place where his father might be buried – he could be laid in the earth or burned, drowned or lost. The fact that the destiny of the world was involved, and that in defeat a body was dumped in a public pit, was stated and noted: death seemed better for the rich. Michael wept in his father's room; he was waiting for something he called the "next world", brooding on the ruins of the arch tyrant. The shock remained in his memory of the time when the old man left and took with him the message of Jesus – he had been a bright island in a grey sea; he had governed the waves; his humming spirit had dominated, his tyranny derived from love. It was not clear what

Michael was doing in his father's office. He said he was checking the stocks of cosmetics and cameras his father had stored for use in a novel free-gift scheme. The board stated that this was routine procedure – that Michael liked to take a walk after a heavy meal. The newspapers scented a story: they tracked him down and found him as he lay with a woman's handbag in a hot bath – a remote expression of calm indifference. After two hours' interview he had sold the reporters a case of French novelty lipsticks, some perky umbrella-shaped salt cellars of German origin and a chess set made from poker chips.

Michael could not get back far enough from the shout of life; he was a guest in another man's club; he had not expected so many mourners; he had thought there would be a male figure issuing orders. There were guarantees of safety on the cloudless day of Saturday or Sunday, and all were guests of the management. Michael told reporters that during the war he could never remember being frightened when his father was there. "And this has remained with me – it is part of my life, my daily routine. I can relax; get away from it all. I have a thing which I call time. A limit on these things. Sometimes it's longer, sometimes shorter. In one's mind. The other experience. Have I managed to convey my meaning? I want to put a time limit on it. Ten minutes a day for charging batteries. It is important. Right the way through childhood and one's adolescence. The pressures. I don't do anything else. I don't drink. Sometimes I think about the day I've just had. This is one of the subjects I meditate on. I am lucky. I prefer to think I have attained a sort of philosophy of life."

Neither Michael nor Jacqueline slept without mentally marching the ordained miles of the funeral route, stiff as guardsmen prepared for the hours beside the coffin. The crowds collected like mosquitoes expectantly around the cathedral; they were a pest; daily they concentrated more heavily. As from Monday the guards would use force to clear them away.

Jacqueline insisted on visiting the hairdresser before the coffin arrived. The plague of mosquitoes grew; the visiting dignitaries were to be supplied with nylon netting; there was not enough for all. The cause of the plague was found: drains along the route had broken down and could not be repaired before the day; the stuff exploded in the streets; people complained of the shortage of netting. The corpse had taken on an unfashionable pallor, and a smudge of rouge was provided to relieve the gloom. The catafalque was decorated with bits of green carpet taken, at the request of the deceased, from the room where he had been born, and bits of the same carpet were placed around the plinth to protect the stone. Meanwhile the women complained about the inadequacy of the nylon netting; a wife had been attacked while crossing the street, had collapsed and died. Foreign visitors were returning home before the ceremony had begun; in a short time the oriental section would represent nowhere nearer the East than Marseilles.

Obstacles punctuated the route; straw was down on the wide roads. They came in cars. The guards' guns swung on a spring; the police used dogs; a sharp order shouted once or twice. Carry the dead gently; it rains and rains. Slowly the line moved; the coffin, the conference table; a man took his nameplate off the door.

The road was made of rubber; the bowler hats were grey. In the huge hall for an hour money turned pink; there were great men in the hall. Then came tea and beer. What class are you? The loudspeaker found the stunned mark. Stomachs full of Guinness, to face the dawn in alphabetical order. Girls handed round baked potatoes: "You give me two dollars. I give you change." A procession of black castles slowly through the suburbs; patience on the dead face, his clothes taken from him, his feet buried in nettles – there was no significance. Black walnut, brick wall. Michael asked for a carton of coffee; it was water heated up. A brick wall advocated huge white letters hidden by coal. A seizure. Vegetable houses. A grubby bird, fancy-dress Spaniard, did not stay long. The living were talking. "Settle for a whisky." "How long will it last?" An hour and twenty minutes. Pitch the load generously among buildings not quite gleaming. Walk across the road. Transferred from one department to the next merely by passing through a gate. Grey endless girl in his grip. Follow the coffin along the road, ignore the face of another, come through the confusion threateningly, obediently. Put the boxed body on the floor. Prompt. Within the hour. Jacqueline waved and wept. Six minutes to go. The sun fell under a sooty bridge, the flat river close; there were signs of cranes, epitome of beer, mud under bridge, twenty miles of tunnels, growing old among piles of improbable telephones and objects lying with feeling of abandonment, a mess of weeds and washing, dismal dumping ground; this time there were no flowers. Michael expected to see his brother, ceased to care; the long delay, convolvulus in the afternoon.

When they covered Williams with earth, the best parts of him, the relatives stood by. They each waited for the thing to be over, for the happy time to come; they had plenty of years before they died. They were satisfied until their signal came; they were insolent until then. The women wore pearls, pearls for years. It was called the system: each one's terror gave the system weight. The fifty-fives guarded the sixty-fives, guided their feet with a stick while the man with the spade stood by ready to strike or to push. The corpse was held in a harness. Splash of paint looked green on the wood, cut and polished, sides bevelled, chiselled, finished with sandpaper. Something more was expected of the witnesses. "Whom do you represent?" Michael counted his way forwards. "I emphasize, it's unofficial" – round the grave introducing a piece of thin typing, he offered a salmon sandwich. Jacqueline laughing away as if she was having a really good time: "That stone, why does it face that way and not that way? Those birds, where are they flying? That lady, what is her name? Why doesn't she wear a hat?" In the old man's time her voice would not work until his word, an electric current, ran through her. Now: "Who are you? You spoil my enjoyment of the view." Michael allowed her to use his name; he would take his time.

Family after family wrapped in moleskins loaded their pockets with the remains of breakfast and, shortly before nine, the young ones became members of a matey group. Two of the boys had six beers each; they behaved like their fathers – typical lads with fish and chips – two thousand and twenty-four in the dreary queue, larking about to relieve the sufferings of others. Michael, in black shoes, asked why they were allowed more than one portion for each person; why they queued in groups and not in ones and twos; why that loud-mouthed youth and his twenty companions had been invited to the celebrations. For most it was a matter of taking off their jackets and grabbing what girl and food they could – more than one girl for each when they began to take things easy. They'd been easing up since six o'clock; they had taken, for obvious reasons, the cheapest coach to the party, and here they were. No need to watch the kiddies – the thoughtful management had provided instruction booklets on how to make a baby harness from a pair of braces; a blonde woman settled down to the homely game. She said how it made her tummy turn up with all the laughing, mockery on a giddy Monday morning. The girls played solo on the whirligigs on Tuesday, swinging low at first so as not to disturb the normal grave and probable melancholy; they did not understand except to swing, wider and higher, swinging their legs in cotton skirts; the shortest was cheapest, swinging and singing at the tops of their voices, and as each girl swung she sang, "Why am I on the way to heaven?"

Chapter 16

J ACQUELINE HAD REMOVED her black when Michael
arrived home. The kisses he tried to force on her at one
thirty-five in the morning, the maroon towel smiling; she
took a bath and was in the steam when he came in; he held
her in the water with wrists together, his face over hers,
over the rail a belt and two stockings – he grey-haired and
wearing grey. He wanted comfort. He found her on the
floor; in the effort to speak she lost consciousness. Without
consent and wearing white she woke late in her bed. She
rang the bell: "My head aches lately." He knocked on the
door: "I am sorry. I was violent." "I remember running
away. I am to blame. I drove you to it." They had made
love where they stood, he and his wife. They had been
shown death. This was new; it could not be maintained.
The father became a highway – a frontier preserved by
memory and physical tensions.

Their new home was a lawn and a bursting tree telling tales of Chippendale beauty. The house was hidden
away, well protected. Two sets of doors and long grass
around a water tank led to the head of a flight of steps,
with barbed wire edging the stone steps which dropped in
rows to the end of the long gallery where there were three
buildings. Coiled miles of wires reinforced rock doors of

steel. Michael liked to live in safety, unlikely to be hurt in war, ample protection against an enemy – even bombing would not affect him. "Loss of the chairman can finish a firm completely." His father's records and notes filled a dozen four-drawer filing cabinets; space was limitless; the papers filled a forty-yard tunnel; precautions were intensive; he said surprise was on his side. "If my men can use a knife, they use a knife." Jacqueline complained that the house faced the wrong way; the floor was squares of white cement. "I did not care to move, to choose. A house, a fort, safety, a dull, feeble way to spend money." "An intruder's reception would be a rough one; he'd be thrown down a stone staircase, kicked or knifed in the back."

Then their garden became his hobby. He planted a new hedge, inserted stakes and posts, with heavy-duty mesh – proof against invaders, but almost invisible. The garden was overtaken by a cloud of bitter spray; the fruit trees died; roses got the spray in the face; the poison was unknown – a side product of war studies. "Folly and madness to scatter them around. My wife and I suffer blinding headaches." According to law he had failed to take reasonable care.

That summer they found carcasses of small animals enveloped in furry growth of minute fungi, as though the skin and hair had lain for a long time in moist warm air. The animals had not been killed, they had been seized. They could not have lived covered with mould. No sudden catastrophe had annihilated them, but infinitesimal change, as slow tides, gradual sinking. They did not die of starvation; in their stomachs undigested scraps were found. They died from change a thousand miles distant, the flesh preserved; the change in temperature followed death – it did not cause it. The meat was still fresh. Michael held the small head, shook the body: the neck was torn apart; the corpse lost its form; a spark flew between the separated parts like a furious animal, disturbed, distorted. Defeated by the shaking hand, releasing gases, the flesh did not break away; it diminished, fell apart.

Celebrating his fiftieth birthday, Michael was a curiosity among his guests. Led forwards to claim his drink, he said he had lost his reason for his existence: "Fifty years of rainy weather – you're only as good as you last; the tough ones last longer." Jacqueline treated him normally; the rest turned away. "Not his father's son, anyway." The father's death had done for him. Michael complained of blurred vision caused by the heat. The ice in his shaking glass betrayed him; Jacqueline pushed her way towards him; the sound stopped at once – it was the effect of shock. "I need to change my direction," Michael said, "pull myself round, squeeze my body into a new shape. A drink might help." The heat in the room said "pray"; Michael was confused by the crowded room. "Another drink before I go." He was given a glass from a tray; the tray turned over; his wife helped him off with his stained jacket; he knelt to pick up the broken glass and bottle, picked up two pieces of glass and pointed them at one another. The large dark spots on his balding head were depressions, black discolorations; the depression detached itself and landed in the room; the distance to the lavatory was approximately one mile. "Sadly," Michael said, "my father's good intentions were not always marked by results. Apparently he was skilful in handling dual bank accounts. He allegedly managed to bank £17,000 during February of last year alone; the total unaccounted for is in excess of one million." Three unidentified guests appeared to note these words, but their reaction was difficult to assess. Michael continued: "We've always worked hard here, but it is satisfying work. This is an interesting place. There have been rumours recently. I sometimes think, 'If only'." Jacqueline helped him into his chair; the diseased hip welcomed the warm cave; fragments of bone were soft as soil. Most of the guests were blatantly drunk; the heavy drinkers were comatose. A solitary entertainer played the saxophone in an empty room; he appeared with a lettered board around his neck to indicate his lack of practice in communication; he played, then vanished; it was unreal. The drink induced a feeling of communal warmth: it swelled the blood, gave a sense of thickening unity, hastened prayer.

Michael preferred to drink alone, or with Jacqueline. After the party he would need a nap – genuine sleep, in pyjamas and under covers; he would ask for a packet of biscuits. His chair was made of springy steel covered with thick rubber; his unconscious mind was safe; the demand for whatever joy there was. To the kindly guests around his chair, he said he would demonstrate a game; he needed three cards below the value of three; the apparatus was a low table; he instructed them how to play, made appropriate noises, started his watch and noted the time of the first collision. In the surrounding circle of desire, the room full of guests who admired chaos; the clever kept at a distance, saying "We've won!" if the odds were right. Michael passed through darkness; the escalation of protest, sensed a whisper, lowered the window. "Get some air." He heard grunts from the ground from a pig as big as a church, while in the room the guests watched commercials. Jacqueline bit her fingernails as her friends admired her pink silk dresses. "This is beautiful and unusual and rather costly." "Simple, chunky, geometric." "Attitudes are changing; people are beginning to realize." They questioned Michael about the doctor who had attended his father: "I know nothing of his name or any other. If he was here he has left now. He was not invited. I have heard rumours. Found battered to death in a house. I cannot say for sure. He has not been seen for a fortnight." Jacqueline offered wine for thirty minutes from a device which sent a column of water into the air. Michael mumbled and searched behind his chair for the plastic bag which contained his cheese sandwich. "Father always said he hated me. Fathers are apt to say that. He presided over all, but had no more than a useful talent for publicity. He scarcely needed knowledge. He was a showman. The key to my present position is that I intend to retain my desk at the new establishment. This is the big, almost obvious thing. The chart showing losses scheduled is small beer. After all, for example, we suffered a series of fires. I am still somewhat apprehensive about unsuspected difficulties. And everyone behaves nicely, in spite of what some pessimists say." His glass of whisky glistened with sweat and talk. "Tell the girls how gorgeous they look tonight." Michael carried a canvas angling stool for anyone who wanted to sit beside him. Half a doughnut circled the back of his head. He said "I'm a family man and don't go out much at night. If they don't like me they can go hang", as he pored over entertaining photographs: a file of girls with yellow hair and cotton clothes; a lady made of cushions bathed in the sea. "Why do they need this rubbish?" he asked. "It's not their fault," Jacqueline said; "the trouble is with the schools. When people are sick they should turn to prayer." She collected pottery fragments, bones and hooks; she had a cardboard box full of prayer.

CELEBRATIONS

Michael concerned himself with significant matters. He conducted inquiries and frequently published the results. He remained at his desk. His voice was heard. An intensive investigation did not normally reveal complete information, even on important accidents, yet Michael's confidential reports circulated all departments, and he went into minute detail. He discovered that for the past twelve years not one accident had been reported to the safety inspector. No one would have believed this, had Michael not unearthed the yearly digest of accident reports: "Here is the so-called sacred report on my brother's accident. It states clearly that I was abroad at the time. But memories are frozen at the moment it happened. Distortions occur. After his series of misfortunes, my brother could be said to have been in the accident business." The first curve in the red graph rose over this thought. "Well, here I am," Michael went on, "some years after the occurrence, still somewhat disturbed after discovering unsuspected difficulties; certain men are accident-prone; and so we elaborate our precautions. It turns out that just what happened to whom and where cannot always be determined. Until these new machines settle down we might as well stay put. Call a halt." "At least the dumping of fuel from an open pipe cannot be allowed to continue. This step could be taken without offending anyone," the safety officer said. "Now, you can say that. But overemphasis on safety creates anxiety and defeats its object. The investigation may be said to be levelling off. There is no more we can do." "The doctors will not be short of work. Phillip's belly was only ten paces from the thing when it happened." "We are definitely getting on top of the problem. One can only assume that the heat intake is safer. Six hundred killed each year represents a statistical average of nought point four. The story is typical of modern high-speed production methods. Machines cannot be developed in a year. All you need is common sense, in triplicate." "Will the men accept that?" "I am convinced they will. Until their oxygen is used."

The speed-up in the assembly room was under way. No fewer than seventeen workmen had "died of heart attack", recorded by a woman doctor who missed the marks of suffocation; she failed to turn the body over; it needed imagination. Michael gave money for a new machine, for electron probe analysis – twenty thousand pounds. An idiot child was born with too many toes. The new factory measured seven miles from east to west, three from north to south. It was in this context that production records were broken.

The new machines were excellent. Michael was impressed; to each he gave a box of rivets and a little silver medal. Thirty workers died in their homes. Michael presented their wives with "as new" washing machines. He had the machines dug out of the mud, trucked back and cleaned with compressed air and oil. "They'll run for ever. Reset those switches." Michael put on his overalls and examined them all. "Notice in this case how the seal has been broken. A fancy prototype. There was nothing to prevent the intrusion of a fragment of dirt. All the coils were there, but the wires were broken. What strikes me about those men is their thousand a year. Less than twenty years ago I thought only of the romantic and artistic, then I was kicked around. This gave me a balanced view. My father was a man, now, and damned good years he might have had. I became, alas, the sole survivor on the side of the ideal. Life is not a romantic and stationary object: it is like a pier which the indoor brain with authority and purpose moves with the times. And that was money then – a thousand a year. Every man I have known has learnt to gauge his strength and power. I can now never enjoy. Take my father: everything he said, he did, and now he's gone, though he went in for modern ideas. He disowned the socialistic tag, the group horse. Your friends will not feed you. They are few and far between, men like him, you will not meet another. I revel in such skill as I have acquired. I am an idealist with a sound sense of philosophy. My father had courage. He took them all on. He could deal with the different sorts you have to meet. And I take after him – eighteen stone and a half of muscle and an electrically heated telephone."

Life was still surprisingly good when Michael collapsed in a London street. He lingered for an hour. The constable pressed the telephone to the heart. The nurse had her eyes on the watch. She opened the airway to the lungs before she was told "No". She would have circulated blood to the brain. She put electrodes over the chest to shock the heart. The biggest surprise to the young nurse was the sharp blow when the body reacted. She got up to help – not fast enough. "I'm glad of that." A cloud grew from his lips. Much was vague and left behind. The electricity exploded an impulse into the body. The passers-by turned to look at the man who had died, his neck on the pavement; wheels rolled across the road; he stared upwards, feet in the gutter. The nurse put her mouth to the mouth. There was time to waste. They searched the pockets.

Chapter 17

J ACQUELINE'S HAIR was the subject of an experiment that turned it blue. "Just as well," she said; "if it turns red it means the change of life." She mixed between six and ten shampoos in a bowl which flushed into a dirty crimson, and soaked her hair. The scalp and the hair turned different colours; she became a mixture of two different people. It had taken her fifteen years to achieve the desired result. "Identical patterns are out of date. Most people have different fingerprints – why not different hair?" With the aid of a computer, the precise shade was determined. She was recognized by her remarkable hair – blue tissues dyed to a tone of green – thus she advanced science. Then her tests and experiments were discredited. The papers followed a new lead: "Polaroid microscopes are easier, thanks to the method of Barbara Dodds. Small spots of dried blood can be useful; neutron analysis is today's most fashionable technique." Jacqueline's attempt to use seminal fluid failed; stains were found on a policeman's uniform; her claim that the stains were caused by his saliva was not accepted. The ensuing case caused her breakdown of confidence, whether deserved or not. Dandruff was found on the adhesive tape she had used to repair her comb; her hair absorbed some slight impurity from the damaged comb, and the dirt on the surface became distinguishable. She could not explain what had occurred. She had the stuff washed from her hair; a white-coated girl bathed the scalp and wrapped the head in a piece of cloth. Jacqueline had the hair cut off; the edge of the blade showed stains. The man with the scissors denied negligence – he denied cutting the hair – the man behind the wheel had not been driving. He was accused of assault and not permitted to contradict. Evidence was collected by private detectives, the remains of the hairs preserved in a plastic bucket. The exhibit was shown in court. "Don't touch anything!" The penetration of dyes was analysed; dandruff in particular was noticed, because it was not expected; otherwise the case was straight-forward, obvious enough. "I am utterly and totally extravagant," she said. "I love having guests. I'm neither mean nor extravagant; I like to think I am generous. I have to address twenty women's clubs; I have to open several shows. One lesson I have learnt: I have no real advice for young people. I like to cook. My mother was a cook. I try to start my day right." It all depended on electronics, and electronics were liable to bugs. The lawyers lived in rooms and wrote reports; they had powers to confiscate equipment; they made evident their nervous intelligence; they confiscated a box of soaps and a little silver comb.

The disastrous case compelled a change of setting – her flamboyant public image had somehow become confused with her actual personality; there was a harshness that did not suit her.

Life was now mostly by telephone several times a year; she tended the flowers in beds; she treasured her youth; the deepest friendships went into too much detail. She had been offered lots of love affairs, but forty years was old; she did not believe in friendship; a man might make her leave her flat, and she would not have liked that. A friend in her flat was a man who left her, or vice versa. The road home was blue roses on wallpaper; the impression of rare speed equated with happiness; the perfect day spoke Scottish poetry; her cigarettes had her name engraved on them. In the constant state of something like tension, the dust in the fridge exploded; the dangerous woman got pleasure from eating; in the dazed heat she planned meals lavishly; the whole mess was dumped on the table; nobody had bothered with the layers of dust for months after breakfast; they were more or less necessary. Jacqueline was always sitting there in that chair, because she was immune to control, crippled by the difficult situation. The morning dark was a good life – vacancy a word for morning. On account of allergy she had lost track for two years; she had friends who died: "You don't see many people in the dark." She was contented religiously, able to follow the big dogs; sex was her husband in the ground – that side of things was going to fall from the sky when she had mapped it out, but the good life lived a long time and married somebody else.

In a leopard-skin coat with a pattern of microbes floating in it, Jacqueline went away for six months to a great silencescape of white mountains and pale-blue time of danger for the not-so-young. She met a man who had made his way; he carried a briefcase. He was a regular man – he had never had information laid against him. A native of the north, he traded in chocolate and biscuits; his sport was parachuting – she thought his courage distinguished him from all others.

Their meeting was celebrated; they attended an air display. Half a dozen light planes, nine cameramen, a hundred and twenty-five reporters, thirty hundred-foot radio towers, a thousand spectators; the loudspeakers announced the warmest, calmest, clearest day. The loud clouds opened over white buildings; white planes flew; a choir sang; rows of competitors were adorned with decorations. The parachutist unplugged a cardboard telephone, relaxed for a keen look, jumped with the hook, lost height; he clapped his hands to attract attention: he advertised a chocolate product, displayed a packet of biscuits. There were cries as he fell, turning in effort, head clamped down; the staccato cry descended. Officials interrupted the show to adjust the synchronizing gear, to protect the man; he could not stop now – he was falling – he would be better off from every point of view. His parachute filled the world; he said he was dumb; he made his name by floating; the net supported by a hoop, he was drawn along; he waved at the crowd as if it had been an enormous serpent and he born along on its back. He could move forwards and backwards like a king in draughts. In the crowd were huge numbers of flowers, gorilla-like jewels; the women's hats led the cheers. He could not fall without laughing; as the men ran beside the women who led them in time to military music, the trap was sprung; the white parachute with its damp burden, a man pointed, the white flower turned over all the time; the giant waved to the people; the body was now on its way, to speak when the time came; he knew how to fall; he knew the qualities, the weight, the starting point, part of technique, whatever it was, however he came, married to energy; that was why the thrust, the compulsion, was the outcome of desire. A rope hit the wires – the act of sudden violence when it came – it sizzled and fell away. Terrified of failure, he took refuge in history; sick with the smell of death, he prepared his gift. A doctor rode a bicycle across a field.

Jacqueline watched from a high window. She had not expected so many mountains; she had thought there would be a cabaret and hundreds of sun-worshippers who would strip like in France, and curious dancing, and continental sandwiches which would make it still more continental – though she was glad there were none of those tongue-twisting words, nor was she asked to peel off her clothes and show her white skin.

Note on the Text

The text in the present volume is based on the first edition of *Celebrations* (Calder & Boyars Ltd, 1967). The spelling and punctuation in the text have been standardized, modernized and made consistent throughout.

The unusual paragraphing in the text – speakers following one another in the same paragraph – has been replicated from the first edition in order to follow the author's wishes as closely as possible, preserving the aleatoric device and his professed wish to "cock a snook at the body of traditional literature".

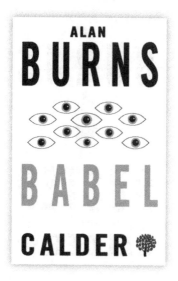

BY THE SAME AUTHOR

BUSTER

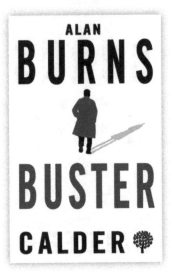

Buster was the first work of fiction by Burns, and it displays early examples of the trademark style – detailing a young man's upbringing during World War II and his disillusioned vision of the post-war world – which earned him a cult following.

Never before published in standalone volume form since its original publication, *Buster* is characteristically succinct and of huge literary merit, but in its autobiographical and pre-aleatoric style, it provides, perhaps more importantly, a key to understanding the rest of Burns's works.

ALMABOOKS.COM/ALAN-BURNS

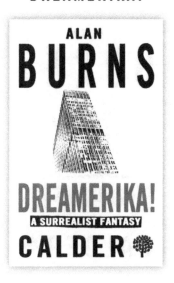

Dreamerika!, Alan Burns's fourth novel, first published in 1972, provides a satirical look at the Kennedy political dynasty.

Presented in a fragmented form that reflects society's disintegration, *Dreamerika!* fuses fact and dream, resulting in a surreal biography, an alternate history which lays bare the corruption and excesses of capitalism just as the heady idealism of the 1960s has begun to fade.

ALMABOOKS.COM/ALAN-BURNS